Goddess Girls

ECHO
THE
COPYCAT

READ ALL THE BOOKS IN THE GODDESS GIRLS SERIES

COMING SOON:

Goddess Girls

ECHO
THE
COPYCAT

JOAN HOLUB & SUZANNE WILLIAMS

Aladdin

NEW YORK   LONDON   TORONTO   SYDNEY   NEW DELHI

ALADDIN

An imprint of Simon & Schuster Children's Publishing Division

1230 Avenue of the Americas, New York, New York 10020

First Aladdin hardcover edition April 2016

Text copyright © 2016 by Joan Holub and Suzanne Williams

Jacket illustrations copyright © 2016 by Glen Hanson

Also available in an Aladdin paperback edition.

For information about special discounts for bulk purchases, please contact Simon & Schuster Special Sales at 1-866-506-1949 or business@simonandschuster.com.

The Simon & Schuster Speakers Bureau can bring authors to your live event. For more information or to book an event, contact the Simon & Schuster Speakers Bureau at 1-866-248-3049 or visit our website at www.simonspeakers.com.

Book designed by Karin Paprocki

The text of this book was set in Baskerville.

Manufactured in the United States of America 0316 FFG

2 4 6 8 10 9 7 5 3 1

Library of Congress Control Number 2016932603

ISBN 978-1-4814-5002-7 (hc)

ISBN 978-1-4814-5001-0 (pbk)

ISBN 978-1-4814-5003-4 (eBook)

We appreciate our mega-fantastic readers!

Keny Y., Koko Y., Paris O., Julia K., Amanda W., Eden O.,
Sydney B., Virginia J., Shelby Lynn J., McKay O., Reese O.,
Ariel S., Emily G., Buu Buu G., Kaitlyn W., Kaylee S.,
Erica B., Madison W., The Andrade Family, Meghan B.,
Kristina S., Caitlynn L., Sarah A., Racheal W., Aubrey B.,
Kathryn C., Ava K., Bryanna G., Jamie E.S., Caitlin R.,
Hannah R., Amy Y., Jasmine R., Sidney G., Aspasia K.,
Abby G., Sarah D., Patricia D., Fe Susan D., Anh M-H.,
Ashley H., Reilly H., Diane G., Daisy S., Ana B., Amelia G.,
Sam R., Anna K., Niki K., Anh H., Christine D-H.,
Khanya S., Micci S., Brianna I., Mackenzie S., Trena J.,
Lillia L., Amanda C., Haley G., Riley G. Renee G., Ellie P.,
Maddie P., Patrona C., Aubrey B., Maria B., Mia T., Alyssa T.,
Lily-Ann S., Laura C., Chelsea G., Megan D., Cassie G.,
Grace H., Lilly T., Lana W., Kristen S., Ally M., Sabrina C.,
Keyra M., Sophie G., Jessica G., Shiresa M.C., Irena G.,
Vivian Z., Emily & the Grondine Family, Hannah H.,
Sydney C., Lily May C., Kira L., Ela N., and you!

—J. H. and S. W.

CONTENTS

1

FirHeart

HIGH IN THE BRANCHES OF A TALL, TALL FIR tree called FirHeart, a twelve-year-old nymph named Echo was getting ready for Nature School. This tree belonged to her and she belonged to it. She had lived in it since she'd been born, here in the forested mountains of Boeotia, Greece, and had even built a small, cute tree house in it for herself.

Most of her tree's branches grew horizontally

outward from its main trunk, which had made it easy to lay boards to form the floor she stood on now. She'd also built herself a table and a shell-lined sink, and had fitted them into the tree's natural curves. Instead of walls, there were handrails on three sides of her small house, with the fourth side left open as an entrance. The pulley-and-vine ladder system she'd made in science class helped her reach the tree house from the ground.

Echo was busy deciding what to wear to class that morning, when a magic breeze carrying a bunch of scrolls whooshed by and tangled long tendrils of her green hair. *Plunk!* The breeze dropped an issue of *Teen Scrollazine* onto the sleeping hammock she'd woven back in fourth grade, causing the hammock to sway gently.

"Thanks!" she called to the breeze. But it had

already whooshed off to deliver scrolls to the two hundred or so other tree houses in this forest. She went over to the hammock, picked up the scrollazine, and unrolled it, planning to take a quick peek before school. Despite its name, the 'zine appealed to all ages, and it mostly carried articles about the immortals who lived on Mount Olympus.

Since this forest was far from Olympus, Echo and her schoolmates never got the 'zine on time. This one was from two weeks ago. Still, everything in it would be new to her, and she would devour the entire thing later tonight. Stuff that happened on Mount Olympus always seemed way more exciting than whatever happened in the forest. In fact, things were kind of boring around here, or so it seemed to her.

She glanced at the main article, which was titled

"Grand Events Planned at the Immortal Marketplace." It was about a big celebration that would be happening soon. Something involving a parade with floats, and then a wedding a couple of days later. Turned out that the parade was actually going to take place this very Saturday, and the wedding on Monday. *Wouldn't it be fun to go?* she thought dreamily. But Mount Olympus was far away, and besides, nymphs like her rarely left their forest. They had to stay and guard their trees.

Alongside the article there was a drawing of Zeus, the Mount Olympus Academy principal, standing next to the beaming couple who were soon to be married. Unfortunately, the bride-to-be wasn't pictured wearing her wedding chiton. Understandable, though. It was considered bad luck to reveal the gown to everyone before the wedding day. Still,

Echo had an interest in fashion and would have loved seeing it.

She noted other details in the drawing. A goat stood beside Zeus, and a honeybee was buzzing around the principal's head. Huh? What was that about? But then, as she unrolled more of the 'zine, her attention was caught by a smaller article that featured a drawing of three MOA students. Apparently they had located something called an herb of invisibility and had won a battle against some giants at the Parthenon. Wow, talk about exciting!

At the left of this drawing was a turquoise-haired mergirl named Amphitrite. The article said she was a Nereid, a sea nymph. There were many kinds of nymphs. And like Echo, most were halfway between mortal and immortal, with limited magical powers.

Echo recognized the girl at the center of the picture right off as the famous goddessgirl of wisdom and inventions, Athena. And the third girl in the drawing was Persephone, the goddessgirl of growing things. Echo gazed fixedly at the chiton Persephone wore. It had a double skirt, and there was a leafy border along its topmost hem. Basically it was the cutest, *evergreenest* outfit ever! In the forest, calling something "evergreen" was an even higher compliment than saying it was mega-cool.

Carefully Echo tore out the drawing of the three girls and tacked it to her bulletin board, alongside oodles of other drawings she'd collected for fashion ideas. She had already copied almost all these ideas when sewing her own clothing. Hmm. There was still a half hour before school. Was that long enough to copy Persephone's design? Yes! If she used the plain green chiton she had planned to wear and simply made a few additions.

Full of enthusiasm for her new project, she grabbed her sewing box, which contained various decorative materials she'd gathered from the surrounding forest and mountains. First she took out a needle made from a piece of shell and threaded it with a long, thin strip of grass fiber. Then she chose some green laurel leaves and pink anemone flowers from her box and sewed them onto the hem of her chiton, making a border just like Persephone's.

All too soon Echo heard other nymphs vining down from their trees to land on the forest floor nearby. Oops! The half hour had passed without her noticing. Wasn't that always the way when you were doing something you loved?

Murmurs filled the forest as each of the nymphs

called out a protective chant to the tree that she lived in and guarded. They renewed these magical chants every morning to keep their trees safe from all possible harm.

Quickly Echo pulled the embellished chiton over her head and twirled in it, feeling like a million stars. Then she styled her hair the way Persephone had done in the picture, tucking leaves and flowers into it here and there. And lastly, she slipped on a pair of strappy sandals, which she'd made out of vines and dyed purple with crushed mulberries a few months earlier. Ta-da! Perfect!

Hearing Daphne, her BFF, Echo peeked down through the branches of her tree. Her friend was with a group of nymphs that included Syrinx, a foreign exchange student visiting their school. Unlike the nymphs in this forest, Syrinx was a

Naiad—a nymph that dwelled in a freshwater river.

"Ye gods! Those chants you guys use are so *yesterday*," Syrinx was exclaiming. "In the river we come up with new ones almost every day!"

This was something Daphne would already know, however. She had once been a Naiad too, before she'd changed herself into a forest Dryad. But Syrinx liked to be a know-it-all.

"I've got dozens of chants. Listen to this one," Syrinx went on.

"Protect this river every day.
Keep it safe while I'm away."

Ooh! Two-line protection chants were hard, and this was a good one, with all the right beats. On the spot Echo decided to copy it. She simply couldn't resist! Of course, she would also say her usual protective spell in case Syrinx's new one didn't work as well. She chanted:

"Protect this fir tree every day.

Keep it safe while I'm away."

"Ready, Echo?" Daphne called up to her from the group of nymphs below. The two of them usually walked to school together. Lately they'd had to include Syrinx, though.

"Coming!" Echo called down. She didn't want to be late. "Guess I'd better make like a tree and leave!" she told FirHeart in farewell. It was their own private joke. Naturally her tree didn't reply. Trees couldn't talk till they were hundreds or thousands of years old, like the ones who taught at Nature School.

Echo stepped into her pulley-and-vine ladder system. All the tree nymphs had them, with hollow-gourd pulleys, and vines strung and looped in a way that balanced a nymph's weight and allowed her to quickly raise herself up or down, depending on which vine she tugged. *Whoosh!* She was on the forest floor in seconds.

She hit the ground a little off balance, however. When she straightened, she came face-to-face with Syrinx. A little rattled, Echo grinned and nervously struck a pose. She raised one arm and lowered her other, copying Persephone's pose on the cover of the 'zine, and hoping she'd look just as fabulous as that goddessgirl. Though she wasn't sure why, she was eager for Syrinx's approval. Maybe because this girl was Daphne's childhood friend and Echo so wanted to be deemed worthy of being Daphne's BFF.

However, instead of admiring Echo, Syrinx giggled and smirked. Then she elbowed one of the other nymphs in the group. "Told you," she said in a loud whisper. Several other nymphs nodded and giggled too.

"Told you what?" asked Echo, her pose slowly wilting.

"Oh, nothing," replied Syrinx. But from the way she and the other nymphs were acting, Echo knew that wasn't true. She felt slighted and a little embarrassed, though she wasn't at all sure what she'd done wrong.

"It's just that we saw the *Teen Scrollazine* this morning too," Syrinx informed her at last. "And I bet the others on the way over that you'd copy something about those three girls in the drawing."

Argh! This nymph is a total leaf fungus! thought Echo. *How mean!*

Luckily, Daphne came to the rescue. "Never mind

that. C'mon, you guys," she said brightly, nudging everyone down the path. Ever since Syrinx had come here, Daphne was always having to smooth things over between the river nymph and Echo, trying to help the two of them get along.

Now, as Daphne and the other nymphs moved off toward school, Syrinx and Echo were left eyeing each other warily. Syrinx slowly tucked a lock of her river-blue hair behind her ear. Without realizing what she was doing, Echo mirrored her action, tucking a tendril of her green hair behind her own ear.

Watching her, Syrinx smiled smugly. Speaking softly so that only Echo would hear, she said: "Ye gods, what a copycat."

Echo's face flushed. With a satisfied air Syrinx hurried ahead to catch up with the others.

At the same time Daphne dropped back to be

with Echo. "You okay?" she asked. A family of deer passed slowly in front of the two girls, causing a gap to form between them and the other nymphs as they all walked to school.

"So, what's wrong with styling my hair like Persephone's and making an outfit like hers?" Echo asked, instead of replying to Daphne's question. "Isn't imitation the sincerest form of flattery?" Just in case Daphne was unaware, she added, "That's an old saying."

Daphne nodded again as they both stepped over a log in their path. "Yeah, I know." She seemed to hesitate for a moment. Then she said, "You might want to be careful. It's one thing to copy our friends' styles. But the gods and goddesses aren't like us. They're super powerful. And the least little thing you do that they don't like could land you in hot water. Remember that mortal girl Arachne?"

"Spider girl, you mean?" The goddess Athena had turned Arachne into a spider when the girl had dared to challenge Athena's weaving skills.

Daphne nodded. "I wouldn't want Persephone to turn you into poison ivy or something for copying her chiton."

"Yeah, or worse, into a *spider* on poison ivy," said Echo. They both giggled. Then with a sideways glance at her BFF, Echo added, "Speaking of bugs, I honestly didn't know it bugged everyone so much when I copied their clothes and stuff. I thought they'd be flattered. Or maybe that they wouldn't even notice."

Daphne twirled a lock of her long blue-green hair around her index finger. Echo started to do the same. Then, realizing what she was doing—copying—she blurted, "I'm doing it again, aren't I? Ye gods!"

Syrinx's voice floated back to them. "'Ye gods'? So now you're copying my buzzwords, too? Get a life, will you, Echo?"

"*You* get a life," Echo whispered in a tight voice. As more nymphs passed by on their way to school, Echo stepped closer to her BFF so their conversation would remain private. "I don't see how you can like that Syrinx," she told Daphne. "I mean, she's *mean*. No one else around here seemed to care what I did till she got here."

Daphne shrugged as the two of them wove among the trees. "She can be a bit much sometimes. But I've known her forever, and it's fun to talk to her about the river and our friends there. I miss the river sometimes, you know? Like you'd miss the forest if you went to live in the ocean or somewhere."

16

"If Syrinx stays here much longer, I might just go live in the sea to get away from her," Echo joked. Then in a more serious tone she added, "I get what you're saying about her, though. And, yeah, I'd miss the forest if I left. But sometimes I do wonder what it might be like to be a different kind of nymph. One who wasn't tied to a tree."

"No way! You'd be miserable. You love FirHeart as much as I love LaurelRing." LaurelRing was the tree Daphne guarded and lived in. "Anyway," Daphne went on, "the rules aren't the same for all nymphs. Naiads can choose to change to a different realm of nymph if they want. But now that I'm a forest nymph, I'll always be one. Because our destinies—like that of all Oreiads, Dryads, and Hamadryads—are firmly rooted among the trees. And there's no changing that."

2

Nature School

As ECHO AND DAPHNE NEARED THEIR SCHOOL, they were startled by a sound and turned to look.

Clink-clink-clink! A herd of white-bearded goats with bells around their necks ran by. The two girls did a double take when one of the goats bleat-spoke from the middle of the herd. "Huh-huh-hurry up, or you'll be la-la-late for school!"

"Did one of those goats just tell us to hurry up?" Daphne asked Echo, her eyes wide.

Just then Pan, the happy-go-lucky godboy of shepherding—and one of the few boys who attended their school—jumped up from the herd so they could see him. "Yeh-eh-ess," he bleated. "I did! Ha! Ha!" He could be a practical joker like that. Laughing, he started herding the girls into the clearing where Nature School met.

"Hey, we're not goats!" Echo scolded him, grinning.

"Uh-huh, I know," he replied, sounding distracted now. His eyes were darting around the clearing. *Probably searching for Syrinx,* thought Echo. For some strange reason Pan really liked that nymph.

His name meant "all." It fit him well, because whatever Pan did, he went *all* out. Usually he was *all* about making and playing musical instruments. Lately, however, he was *all* about crushes. It seemed that he liked a different girl every few days. So far none of them had liked him in return, though. Most couldn't see past the goofy way he bleated his words. Or the fact that he had pointy ears, two goat legs, and a goat tail.

Echo felt protective toward him, especially knowing he was now crushing on Syrinx. That mean river nymph had made it quite plain she didn't return his affection. And she hadn't been very nice about it either.

Still, Pan didn't give up easily. Echo watched him take a small bunch of daisies over to the Naiad nymph and present them to her. "Roses ah-ah-are red, violets ah-ah-are blue. I've got flowers 'specially for you," he bleated.

"Tha-a-anks," Syrinx bleated back in a mocking way.

Pan's cheeks turned red. Whether from pleasure at Syrinx's accepting his flowers, or from embarrassment at her imitation of him, Echo wasn't quite sure. It wasn't his fault that he sometimes sounded like a goat. Being part goat, he just couldn't help it!

The minute Pan turned to go find a seat, Syrinx tossed the flowers to the ground. "Did you see that?" Echo said to Daphne, annoyed on their friend's behalf.

Daphne sighed. "Just try to deal, okay? Syrinx is only here for another week. C'mon. We're going to be late."

Echo gritted her teeth. "I'll try."

They both entered the misty clearing that served as their classroom. It was big enough to seat all two hundred or so students who lived in their forest. Eight ancient magical trees ringed the clearing and taught them different topics. Students had nicknamed the trees "treechers," as in "tree" plus "teachers."

As her classmates also took their seats, Echo sat down cross-legged on a red-capped toadstool dotted with big white spots, then scooched over so Daphne could sit beside her. But just then Syrinx looped an arm through Daphne's and steered her to go sit on a pillow of thick, floating mist only big enough for two. Whatever! Once Syrinx went back to her river, things would return to normal again, Echo reminded herself. Hopefully the other nymphs would no longer be under the spell of her mean personality then and would remember they were actually Echo's friends.

"Good morning!" chorused the eight treechers once everyone was seated. They were Hamadryads, some of them thousands of years old. It was hard to imagine they had once been young nymphs like

Echo and her friends, flitting around the forest. Over the centuries, they had grown ancient and wise and had chosen to meld with their trees forever. Which meant that their faces now appeared on the upper part of their trunks. And their many branches had become their arms, a protective canopy that could shield the classroom from occasional bad weather. All eight had put down deep roots, content to stay here in this clearing and share their wealth of knowledge with younger nymphs for all time to come.

Class began, and the treechers introduced the day's assignment, each taking turns to speak. Since the treechers ringed the clearing, students had to constantly twist their heads to face whichever tree was speaking.

"Today you are to embark on a foraging project,"

announced Ms. Karya, a hazelnut tree. She waved her nut-covered branch arms toward the surrounding forest to indicate the area in which they'd be working.

Unlike the rooted treechers, students spent a lot of time roaming the forest on their own. The philosophy of Nature School was that most learning should take place in the world outside and involve lots of observation and doing. Still, there were in-class assignments now and then, and graphite rock styli and slates were available for note taking. (And for doodling fashion ideas when the treechers weren't looking.)

"Your assignment is to create a protective suit of armor using found objects. Each of you will return here by the end of the day, wearing your project," said Ms. Ptelea, the elm tree.

"And you should be prepared to tell the class how and from what dangers your costume might protect you," said Ms. Balanos, an oak tree.

"Protect us," Echo murmured, pretty much repeating the treecher's last two words.

"For instance, from sickness, weather, et cetera," Ms. Morea explained. "You must study forest plants and creatures carefully today. Observe how they protect themselves, and base your armor on that." An olive tree with slender silvery-green leaves, Ms. Morea was rumored to be three thousand years old. She was Echo's favorite treecher of all.

"Isn't basing our work on something the same as copying?" Echo asked her now, feeling confused.

"You ought to know," Syrinx whispered to her from her mist bench one toadstool over. Daphne murmured something to Syrinx, looking embarrassed by the girl's unkind comment. But a few other nymphs had overheard and giggled.

"Everything under the sun has already been done," Ms. Ampelos, a hundred-foot-tall grapevine, replied to Echo's question. "All inventions are built on the shoulders of older ones. So be yourself, but feel free to borrow ideas from nature."

"If you put your stamp on whatever you do, you can make it your own. Understand?" added the popular poplar tree, Ms. Aigeiros.

No, Echo did not understand. To "make something her own" totally seemed like copying. What was the difference between the two? She just didn't get it! Plus, she didn't have the first idea how to invent armor. When she shrugged uncertainly, it sent Syrinx into a new fit of giggles, which the river nymph quickly turned into pretend coughs.

Ms. Morea stared from one girl to the other, the bark rippling above her eyes into frown lines. Obviously sensing some trouble between Echo and Syrinx, she gestured her branch arms to call them over. "Girls! Olive branch, please!"

Oh nuts, thought Echo. This meant she and Syrinx were being called up for a moment of personal friend-ship counseling. With an inward sigh she reluctantly stood, and both girls went to stand before the treecher.

A few leaves fluttered to the ground as Ms. Morea's branches circled the girls' shoulders, so that the three of them could have a private talk. Her big brown eyes studied them from below her bark-brows. "Now, what's the problem, nymphs? I sense tension."

"Oh, it's all good," Syrinx said, fake-smiling at the treecher. "We were just teasing. An inside joke. Right, Echo?"

"Um, yeah," Echo replied. Syrinx might be a brat and a bully, but for Daphne's sake especially, Echo didn't want to make this into a big thing. So no matter how much the treecher prodded, neither girl would admit that anything was wrong. In the end the two nymphs simply clasped the olive branch together in the traditional way of making up at school. As if that would erase the tensions between them and make them instant friends.

No way! thought Echo as they returned to their seats. She couldn't wait for Syrinx to go back to her river.

"Now, class," sing-songed Ms. Kraneia, a cheery cherry tree. "This is to be an individual assignment. No teams allowed."

Ms. Syke the fig tree added, "Your work is due here at sunset today. We won't give a fig about excuses.

No 'the deer ate my homework' or 'the woodpeckers pecked my project.'"

With that the treechers commenced speaking the daily pledge, and all the student nymphs joined in:

> *"Tread gently today,*
> *Among flower and fern.*
> *Nature's our gift,*
> *And from it we learn."*

As their words died away, Echo and the other nymphs stood and left the circle to tackle the assignment they'd been given. Since teams weren't allowed, she and Daphne waved bye. Then everyone spread out in different directions to search for objects they could turn into armor.

Echo departed the clearing and moved through

the forest. There, birds swooped through the olive, fir, and cypress trees around her. White and yellow butterflies flitted about on flowers and low-growing bushes. They even settled on her hair now and then. But she was so focused on coming up with an armor design, she hardly noticed.

Spotting a black-and-white goliath beetle in her path, she crouched to study its armorlike exoskeleton. If she based her project on this beetle, she'd have to gather a bunch of insect shells together to make armor big enough to fit her. Is that what her treechers meant for her to do? It would mean killing a lot of bugs for their exoskeletons, and she wasn't up for killing even one! After all, their pledge to "tread gently" was all about not harming stuff. She stood and moved on.

In search of more ideas, Echo wandered farther

from school, thinking hard about how armor worked. Trees had bark to protect them. No way would she peel off a tree's bark and use it as armor for herself, though. That would leave the poor tree defenseless against disease and bugs and other harmful things. Besides, bark armor would be super itchy and rough, not to mention heavy.

A cone fell from a pine tree onto her foot as she was walking. *Hey!* She picked it up and studied it. Pinecones protected the seeds within them. That was sort of like armor. After quickly weaving a bag from dried grasses, she began collecting any cones she found here and there on the dappled forest floor, hoping she'd figure out a way to make armor out of them.

Eventually she wound up in an area called the Forest of the Beasts. It was about one mile away from

Nature School, but many more miles from Mount Olympus Academy, the school that goddesses and gods attended.

She had been here before. Every other Tuesday, Zeus allowed the forest nymphs use of this area to study its different beasts. In their last Tuesday class, they'd practiced blending into the surrounding woods to avoid detection by the monstrous creatures here. The beasts in this forest weren't real, though. They were only mechanical copies of actual beasts that roamed Earth. Still, the beasts were scary-looking and could be dangerous!

A sudden gust of wind chilled the air. "I smell rain," Echo said aloud. Wet weather wouldn't cancel their class assignment. But if the rain turned heavy, the treechers would give students more time to complete the project. Which was only fair, since rain made it hard to see well and too muddy to move about easily. She could definitely use another day. One-day assignments like this one could be, well, beastly!

Just then Echo was surprised to see a great flash of bright light. She waited for a rumble of thunder to follow. It didn't. That was odd. Then, hearing voices, she went still. People were somewhere nearby! She crouched low, out of sight amid some ferns, her brown eyes searching her surroundings.

Sometimes MOA students came to the Forest of the Beasts to practice their archery and battle skills. The Forest was off-limits to nymphs when they came. Were they here now? Wait, this was Wednesday, and MOA students normally only came on Fridays. So who . . .

The skies opened up and began to sprinkle. Quickly the rain became harder, pelting her. Echo didn't mind and knew the other nymphs wouldn't either.

They were used to being out in all kinds of weather. Still, she blinked when there was another flash of light. Again, no thunder. Weird!

When it looked like a real storm was brewing, she loped for home with her bag of pinecones, forgetting all about the voices she'd heard earlier.

As the lightning increased, she picked up her pace. She sensed other nymphs in the forest doing the same, and saw them moving among the trees now and then.

Because trees were tall, they were targets for lightning. And the sap running through them made them good conductors of electricity if lightning did strike. It was said that mortals avoided the forest in storms because it could be a dangerous place to take cover. But nymphs didn't have to worry about such things. Their spells kept them and their trees safe.

Uh-oh. Her spell! She'd meant to chant her usual one after she'd copied Syrinx's spell earlier this morning, but she'd been in such a hurry that she'd forgotten. Would Syrinx's spell have the same protective power as her own? A bad feeling stirred inside Echo. A feeling that something was about to go terribly wrong. Heart pounding, she raced like the wind for home.

3

Ka-BOOM!

WHEN ECHO WAS JUST TWO DOZEN STEPS FROM
her FirHeart, she breathlessly called out the chant
she'd forgotten to say that morning:

> *"Protect this tree.*
>
> *Let no ax chop it.*
>
> *Should trouble come,*
>
> *Let my spell—"*

Ka-BOOM!

"–stop it!"

Echo finished the first part of her chant in a desperate shout, striving to be heard above the loud cracking sound. But it was too late. A lightning bolt had struck her tree! The bolt seemed to slide sideways out of the forest itself, instead of straight down from the sky.

Oomph! The force of the electric pulse tossed her backward into a pile of leaves. She pushed up on her elbows, watching in horror as her tree split from its lower trunk as if chopped at the base by that ax in her tardy chant. Only, this ax was made of lightning!

Her tree tilted sideways. *BAM!* It slammed to the ground, narrowly missing her and the nearby trees that were homes to her classmates.

"FirHeart!" she yelled in agony. Although trees couldn't speak, there was an emotional bond between them and their nymphs. A bond that had suddenly been broken by a bolt of lightning! She leaped up from the pile of leaves and fought her way through dense branches that angled every which way out of the downed tree. The bolt had cut deeply, exposing the hardest, strongest wood—the heartwood. Even if her tree hadn't fallen, it was damaged so badly that it would soon become food for insects.

Echo's own heart twisted in her chest as she sadly counted the twelve rings that showed her tree's age. Although FirHeart had stood fifty feet tall, it had only been twelve years old, the same age as her. Trees with nymphs to protect them grew much faster than other trees. However, she hadn't been much of a protector, had she? She turned away, unable to bear looking at the scarred, splintered remains lying in the leaves.

After pushing her way back through twisted branches, she kneeled down alongside what was left of her tree. A stump.

Other nymphs soon gathered around. One by one and in groups, they arrived on silent feet. She heard them murmuring among themselves in shock and dismay.

A hand was rubbing her back. Daphne had come. "This is awful! I don't get it," her BFF said. "Your morning chant should have protected your tree. None of ours were hurt."

A long moment passed. Then Echo admitted, "I didn't say it. I tried a new one instead."

"You changed your chant?" Daphne asked in scandalized disbelief. Those around Echo gasped and drew back.

"Syrinx said she changes her river chants all the time," Echo said, defending herself.

Syrinx rolled her eyes. "Don't blame this on me. I never suggested you try the same."

The other nymphs whispered among themselves, their eyes accusing.

"That copycat . . ."

"How could she . . ."

"Her poor tree . . ."

They were right. Not saying her chant had been devastatingly careless. If only she could turn back time.

Of all the nymphs, only Daphne offered Echo a hug and a few words of comfort. Echo could tell that the others blamed her, just as she blamed herself. Nymphs were supposed to guard and protect their trees, to deflect lightning and disease and harsh weather and fire and all sorts of other trouble.

"I'm sorry, FirHeart. So sorry." Echo hugged the splintered stump of her tree tight.

As the storm began to rage again, the other nymphs scattered to their trees. "Come on. You can stay with me in LaurelRing," Daphne offered kindly.

"No," Echo said, shaking her head. "I won't abandon FirHeart, even if he is just a stump with roots now." Plus, she didn't want to be around that smug Syrinx, who was already staying with Daphne. "You go. Protect your tree. In case another bolt comes," she told her friend. Everyone knew that when nymphs were in residence, their presence offered their trees extra protection.

"Okay, but I'll be back," said Daphne as she withdrew.

Echo was so distraught that she hardly noticed when rain sheeted down on her.

Sometime after the storm passed, she heard footsteps approaching. Daphne and Pan had brought her some food, but she refused to eat. Night came, and still Echo sat by FirHeart's stump. Though the bond between her and her tree had been broken, she hoped that her presence was still a comfort to FirHeart in some small way. She fell asleep with her head lying upon his thick roots, which spread out from the base of the stump.

The next morning the sun warmed her fallen tree, and soon the sweet smell of fir needles and sap filled the air. While the other nymphs went off to school, Echo spent the day clearing away broken branches and stacking any unbroken tree house floorboards she found. She also gathered bits and pieces of her belongings from the ground, including the ladder vines she'd woven and some of her clothes. Her fashion drawings were mostly ruined, but she set those that weren't out in the sun to dry.

When she found the waterproof mat that had served as her tree house roof, an idea came to her. Before she knew it, she had begun to build a little hut on the ground right next to FirHeart's stump, from the pile of branches and floorboards she'd saved.

After school Daphne and Pan came over and pitched in to help her finish off the simple hut. When Pan left, Daphne insisted that she and Echo eat dinner together in the hut, and Daphne even brought Echo some food and household items, such as eating utensils carved from twigs, plates made from shells, and a pillow stuffed with dried grass.

Once they'd eaten the veggie pie and berries Daphne had brought, Pan came back to hang out. He quickly fashioned a new musical instrument out of one of FirHeart's brown cones and attempted to play it. Echo could tell he was trying to boost her spirits.

"Honest opinion," he said when he finished a tune. "Was that good enough to get me into Apollo's band?" This was Pan's dream. To someday play with the godboy of music's group, Heavens Above.

Echo and Daphne didn't say anything. Plagued with thoughts about her loss of FirHeart, Echo had barely been listening.

"No, huh?" he said, sounding a little deflated. "If only I could come up with a great new instrument. Something with a fantastic sound."

"It'll happen," Daphne reassured him. "Just give it time."

Echo knew she should chime in with some encouragement too. But she was still too wounded to think about anyone but herself.

And then a plan began to take shape in her mind. Maybe all was not lost. Maybe the treechers could help. When Daphne and the other nymphs returned to their trees at sunset and Pan left for his home on the outskirts of the forest, Echo slipped from her hut, entered the school clearing, and went straight to Ms. Morea.

"I'm glad you've come. I heard about FirHeart, and I'm so sorry," the treecher said gently. She opened her branches wide, and Echo ran into them for a hug.

Stepping back after a minute, Echo explained to the treecher how she'd used Syrinx's chant, thinking it would protect her tree. And how it hadn't.

"I see," said Ms. Morea. "Well, because rivers change and flow, the chants that protect them must change often too. However, trees are stable and solid and forever. Therefore, our tree chants must be so as well."

"Oh," said Echo. It was like what Daphne had said

about how Naiads could change into other kinds of nymphs if they wanted to, but Oreiads and Dryads like her and her friends couldn't. Ms. Morea was wrong about trees being forever, though. FirHeart wasn't. A tear ran down Echo's cheek. "I just wanted to ask if you could maybe somehow fix FirHeart?"

At this, all the treechers' branches rustled, a sad and lonely sound. The other seven had been listening in on her conversation with Ms. Morea, and now all eight ancient trees spoke as one. "We're sorry," they chorused. Sometimes they spoke this way, all together, especially when there were important matters at hand.

"Please?" Echo begged, looking around the circle. "It wasn't till I lost my tree that I realized just how much I loved it. I thought it would always be there for me, but . . ."

The treechers gazed at her with sympathy as she

rushed on. "If you fix FirHeart, you could give him to someone else who'll take better care of him if you want to." It wrenched her heart to say that, but she'd do anything to save her tree.

"We do not have the power to make it so," chanted the eight trees.

Echo continued to argue the matter. But it was clear the treechers could do nothing for her.

"Couldn't you give Echo another tree to guard?" pleaded a new voice. It was Daphne. She'd silently come into the clearing and now moved forward to join her friend. "Echo meant well. She loves FirHeart. We all make mistakes."

The treechers shook their branches from side to side. "A tree is a once-in-a-lifetime gift."

But then Ms. Morea cocked her upper branches as if she'd had an idea. "Unless . . . Maybe Zeus would agree to make an exception?" she mused aloud.

The other trees gasped. "You would take this to Zeus?"

Ms. Morea nodded with an up-and-down movement of her branches. "He's not only principal of Mount Olympus Academy, after all. He's also King of the Gods and Ruler of the Heavens."

The other treechers looked doubtful, but in the end they said, "We will consider the matter. If it seems right, we will send word to Zeus at MOA. You may go now, girls."

Echo and Daphne thanked the treechers. They'd been kind after all, even if they hadn't been able to bring FirHeart back to life.

"That's something anyway," Daphne said, sounding encouraged by the treechers' offer as the girls departed the clearing.

"I don't really want another tree, though," Echo told her. "I just want FirHeart back. Even if I have to let some other nymph care for him."

As they headed home, Daphne kept trying to convince her that all would be well—that the treechers would convince Zeus to let her have another tree. After a while Echo tuned her out. Her friend just didn't seem to understand that her heart ached for her tree and her tree alone. *Where is home now?* she wondered. Was she doomed to live in her hut forever? With FirHeart's stump a steady reminder of her carelessness?

Halfway back to her hut and what was left of FirHeart, she finally tuned back in to Daphne. "But if Zeus could give you a new tree . . . ," she was saying, still trying to convince Echo that this would be a good thing.

Echo stopped in her tracks. Because an idea had just struck her, as hard and fast as lightning had struck FirHeart. "Zeus! That's it!"

"Huh?" asked Daphne.

"This is all his fault!" Echo declared. "Don't you get it? Zeus controls lightning and thunder. He must've been riding his white-winged horse, Pegasus, above our forest yesterday morning, and carelessly flung a bolt at my tree! Probably just on a whim. I bet he doesn't even know or care what he's done. Ruined my life—that's what!"

Daphne's forehead wrinkled in thought. "Suppose the bolt did come from Zeus. What can you do about it?" She shrugged. "The gods do as they please."

Anger swelled inside Echo, and her hands balled into fists at her sides. "I want my tree back. And Zeus is going to give it to me."

Daphne's eyes widened, but she didn't try to argue. She probably sensed that it wouldn't have done any good.

And indeed, Echo had made up her mind. First thing tomorrow morning she would set out for Mount Olympus. She would go meet with Zeus and see what he had to say for himself. And if she couldn't get satisfaction, she'd try to find a way to make his life as miserable as he had made hers!

4

Narcissus

W HEN THE SUN PEEKED OVER THE HORIZON
the next morning, Echo got up. She put on the
Persephone-style dress she'd made on Wednesday
and washed the previous night, then slipped on
her purple sandals. Since most of her clothes had
been ruined, this was her best outfit now. Once
she was ready to set out for Mount Olympus, she
folded the long edges of the waterproof roof mat

down around the sides of her hut and tied it shut.

She glanced at her tree—or what remained of it, anyway. "You're probably wondering what I'm doing, right?" she asked FirHeart's stump as she hunted around the area for a piece of bark big enough to write on. "I'll be gone for a while. But I'm not abandoning you forever or anything. I'll be back soon. With good news." Although not nearly as sure about that as she made out, she wanted to sound encouraging. And if FirHeart could somehow understand, she wanted him to know she meant to keep her promise to return.

When she finally found some bark on the ground, Echo used a graphite stick to write a message on it to Daphne and Pan: *Be back in a few days. Don't worry.* She didn't explain that she was going to Mount Olympus Academy, or why she was headed there.

Daphne might guess her plan because of their conversation the day before. But by the time Daphne read the note, Echo would be long gone and it would be too late for her friends to try talking her out of confronting Zeus.

She set the note against the door of the hut. "Bye, FirHeart," she whispered at last. "I'll miss you." Then she turned away and moved off through the forest.

As she soundlessly threaded her way among trees belonging to other nymphs, she wondered if anyone else around here would miss her. Besides Daphne, Pan, and FirHeart, that was. The rest of her so-called friends all seemed to be taking Syrinx's side against her lately. Which meant it would take more than an olive branch to set things right among them all.

Echo was a ball of tangled feelings as she traveled onward. She was mad at those other nymphs, mad at herself, and *super*mad at Zeus. Why had he thrown that lightning bolt? Did he know how much trouble it had caused? Well, she was going to insist that he fix things. Just because he was King of the Gods and Ruler of the Heavens, that didn't give him the right to wreak havoc in her life! Nuh-uh, Mr. Thunderpants!

While sidestepping tree trunks and ducking under low-hanging vines, she imagined how their conversation might go. After she scolded Zeus about his errant bolt, she would say, *I demand that you restore FirHeart to life!* Realizing the error of his ways, Zeus would become apologetic and reply, *You're right. Please forgive me. Even the King of the Gods can make mistakes. I will do as you ask.*

Of course, she wasn't exactly sure how she'd get into the Academy's main building after she reached it. Like everyone else, she knew it was located at the top of Mount Olympus. And she'd seen drawings of it in *Teen Scrollazine,* but none had been comprehensive. For all she knew, it had a high wall and a moat around it. Somehow she'd figure out how to get inside once she got there.

Echo had left her forest and was somewhere in the middle of the Forest of the Beasts when she heard something unusual. Stopping, she cocked her head to listen. Voices again. Someone was coming!

She leaped behind a eucalyptus tree, just in time to watch some mortals disappear into an intricate maze of leafy hedges known as the labyrinth. She didn't see how many people there were, but one had been carrying an artist's easel. And she could tell they were mortals because their skin didn't shimmer the way that of immortals did.

What were they doing here? Fools! There were signs

posted all around the Forest of the Beasts, saying the area was off-limits to mortals.

Even she and her friends had never dared to venture into the labyrinth itself. The treechers had warned them that there was some sort of fantastical beast-making machine at the center of it, one specially designed to spawn opponents for the immortal students to practice battling. Although nothing could kill immortals, she'd seen enough of the beasts in this forest to know they could still cause immortals extreme discomfort.

She was in a hurry. Still, she couldn't just let those unsuspecting mortals go into the most dangerous part of the Forest without checking that they'd be okay. They might get mangled by a beast, or worse!

Moving after the group, Echo silently entered the labyrinth. Two dozen tricky turns later, she found

her way to its center. There she discovered a courtyard with a gurgling pool where hollow reeds, bright
white flowers, and colorful lilies grew.

From the mouths of a three-headed dragon fountain in the middle of the pool, water sprayed merrily,
and then dripped back down the dragon's scaly body.
Fantastic plants wiggled and writhed below the trees
bordering the courtyard. And because the trees'
umbrella canopy threw deep shadows, it seemed like
early evening here instead of morning.

The mortals had reached the far side of the pool.
She was surprised to see that there were only two of
them—a girl and a boy, both about her age—since
she'd thought she'd seen more before. The girl sat
on the short stone wall around the pool. She had set
up her easel to sketch, while the freckled mortal boy
studied her work. Their attention was mostly focused

on a statue of a boy in a short tunic, wearing a metal breastplate over his chest. Echo couldn't see the front of the statue from where she stood, but its arm was raised and frozen in the act of throwing a spear, and the artist seemed to be drawing a picture of it.

Too bad I can't borrow that statue's armor for my school assignment and somehow "make it my own," thought Echo. Then she wondered if completing the assignment even mattered. She wasn't sure how much longer she'd be allowed to attend Nature School, now that she didn't have a tree to care for anymore. Would she be kicked out? A lump came into her throat.

Seeing no monsters nearby, she was about to tiptoe away, when the boy statue suddenly moved. And spoke, too!

"Hare!" it said. Echo looked around, expecting to see a big rabbit hopping through the courtyard.

Instantly the freckled boy leaped up and ran over to the statue to restyle its already perfect *hair*. She grinned to herself, realizing her hare/hair mistake. She also realized that the talking statue was actually a real mortal boy. So there were *three* mortals here in the labyrinth.

"Hold still, Narcissus!" the artist told the posing boy.

Time to go, thought Echo, seeing that all was okay. But when the not-a-statue boy named Narcissus turned his head toward his friends and smiled, she froze, her mouth falling open. Not because she was worried that she'd been spotted, but because she'd caught a glimpse of Narcissus's face.

His eyes! They were the color of a sparkly blue waterfall. His teeth flashed white. And his jaw was square and strong. He looked, well, noble. She'd seen plenty of immortal boys in the 'zine and the

Greekly Weekly News before. Mega-cute ones like Poseidon, the godboy of the sea, and Ares, the godboy of war. Yet she was instantly sure that Narcissus had to be the . . . Cutest. Boy. *Ever!*

Her heart began to beat fast. Was this what it felt like to fall in like with a boy? Many of her fellow nymphs had been boy crazy for some time, but Echo had never crushed before. Unless you counted being starstruck for about twenty minutes one afternoon when she'd seen a picture of an actor named Orion on a drama poster that had randomly blown into her forest.

But then she'd heard he was kind of mean to the goddessgirl of the hunt, Artemis, who had always been kind to nymphs. After that Orion hadn't looked so cute anymore. Mini crush over.

Just then Echo heard a rustling sound. It was so faint that none of the mortals' ears picked up on it.

Peering deep into the shadows, she saw two red dots glowing in the farthest part of the hedge that bordered the whole courtyard. Eyes. Scary ones. The more she stared, the more the craggy features of a metal beast began to take shape. It was a creature she recognized from her Nature School studies—a monstrous serpentine creature called the Drakon Thespiakos!

A bolt of fear speared her. And concern for the safety of these mortals—especially that cute Narcissus. She ran toward the group. "Beast!" she yelled, pointing toward the hedge.

The three mortals all jumped, startled to see her. Then everything seemed to happen at once, really fast. Narcissus backed up, moving closer to the hedge . . . and bumped right into the metal Drakon!

Pzzzt! A shower of small sparks shot from the creature's red eyes. They fizzled out quickly and didn't come anywhere near Narcissus's armor. Still, he tumbled away from the beast and toward the fountain, yelling out in alarm. "Whoa, killer sparks!"

The freckled boy who'd just styled Narcissus's hair yelled, "Watch out, Narcissus! Don't look into the pool, whatever you do!" The boy lunged at Narcissus, knocked him out of the way, and then accidentally fell into the fountain himself, splashing the artist and soaking her roll of drawing papyrus.

Meanwhile, Echo bravely flung herself at the Drakon. *Crash!* It fell to the ground, with her on top of it. She cringed, waiting for it to do some awful magic to her. But luckily, the mechanical beast only clanked a few times, then made a sound like a balloon losing air, and went dead silent.

Narcissus folded his arms and frowned at her, "Well, that stunt pretty much ruined everything."

Instead of thanking her, he and his two friends were now glaring at her!

"But I saved you," Echo told him, sitting up.

"And almost sent him to his doom in this pool," said the freckled boy as he climbed out of the water.

"Doom?" Echo repeated, getting to her feet. The freckled boy nodded.

However, Narcissus rolled his sparkly blue eyes and said, "Whatever, Tiresias." Then to Echo he explained, "He's superstitious. Every time I even glance at a pond or a mirror or a piece of glass—"

"You know the prophecy," Tiresias cautioned Narcissus. Then he spoke to the artist as he used both hands to wring water out of his tunic. "Tell her, Anaxandra."

The artist nodded and then confided to Echo, "Narcissus isn't allowed to look at his reflection, or his heart will disappear into thin air. Poof!"

"Yeah, as in . . ." Tiresias drew a finger across his throat. "No one can live without a heart."

Echo gasped. "You mean it might actually kill you to look at your own reflection?" she asked Narcissus.

"It's just a dumb prophecy." He shrugged, looking unconcerned. As the other two mortals pushed the beast upright again, Narcissus circled it. "We found this mechanical monster yesterday in the Forest and brought it here to use as a prop for sketches of me. Epically cool the way his eyes shot sparks even though the rest of him seems to be turned off. Me pretending to fight him would have made for some dramatic drawings, don't you think?"

Tiresias glared at Echo again. "That was the plan. Until you came along, that is."

She sighed. "Oh! Sorry."

65

"Yeah, well, this beast is toast. So I guess we're finished here," said Tiresias. The mortals began packing up their belongings and preparing to depart.

"Oh, one thing before we leave," said Narcissus, turning back to Echo. "Since I've never seen my reflection in pool or mirror, I ask that everyone I meet offer a few words to describe me. Adjectives. Preferably glowing ones."

"Right, and we record all the adjectives and who said them in his fan scrollbook." The artist pulled from her bag a dry papyrus scroll that was the same blue as Narcissus's eyes. Pen poised, she gazed expectantly at Echo.

"Uh-um," stuttered Echo. Narcissus was so irresistibly *kee-yute* that she wouldn't know where to begin. She felt her face flush.

"It's easy," Narcissus coaxed. "Just say stuff like that

I have amazing hair. Awesome style. Things like that."

"Uh-huh, amazing hair. Style," Echo echoed. It must be hard not to ever, ever be able to see yourself. You'd really want to know what you looked like. So as the artist wrote her words down, Echo quickly excused Narcissus's obvious desire for flattery. It was kind of understandable, really.

Once she'd finished writing, Anaxandra began stuffing her papyrus scrolls in her bag. "I like your chiton," she told Echo.

Pleased, Echo smiled. "Thanks. I made it myself."

Narcissus's face lit up as he suddenly took notice of what she was wearing. "Do you make clothes for guys, too?"

"I've never tried," she admitted.

He smiled, dazzling her. "Well, do you think you could maybe sketch out some outfits for me real quick while the others pack everything up? See, I long to be a model," he informed her.

"A model what?" asked Echo, not understanding. This guy had her so bedazzled, she could barely remember her own name, much less use her brain to understand words.

"A fashion model. You know. Modeling clothes that someone else creates—preferably someone totally talented and famous like Moda. Um, what does that guy call himself again, Tiresias?" Narcissus asked, glancing at the freckled boy.

"A fashion designer," Tiresias supplied easily. He came over to shake Echo's hand. "I'm Narcissus's agent and stylist, by the way. And you are?" He and Narcissus seemed much more interested in her now that they knew she could sew.

"Echo, an Oreiad nymph," she replied.

"Nice to meet you," said Tiresias.

Narcissus turned his handsome face toward her again. "See, if a designer created high-fashion outfits for me, I'd wear them in a runway show. To show them off to rich people who'd buy them. Or copies of them, anyway."

Copies? Echo sure was hearing that word a lot lately. But unlike the nymphs, these mortals seemed to approve of the idea of copying. Well, the idea of copying *clothing*, anyway.

After all that had happened over the past couple of days, Echo needed cheering up. This was just the ticket. These mortals were inviting her to help out with Narcissus's career! She liked fashion. And she was good at it. Maybe having that in common was a sign that she should accept the invitation and try to get to know this boy better. Maybe they'd soon be crushing. Maybe it would turn out they were destined to be together!

But then she hesitated, remembering her plan to visit Zeus. She really needed to get going. Gesturing beyond the labyrinth in the general direction of Mount Olympus, she said, "Well, the thing is, I—"

Before she could finish with "have to go meet someone," a whirring, flapping sound reached their ears.

Tiresias leaped to his feet in alarm. "What now?"

"Another beast?" asked Narcissus. They all looked toward the maze's entrance.

"No, that's the sound of winged sandals. I forgot, it's Friday," said Echo. "Hide!"

"Huh?" said Narcissus.

"Immortal students from Mount Olympus Academy come here on Fridays," Echo explained hurriedly before she jumped behind a strange, wiggly fern. "We shouldn't be here!"

At this, Narcissus perked up. "I'd like to meet some immortals. Maybe they could help my career!" Luckily, his two mortal friends pulled him to hide behind the same bushes as Echo. Just in time, too.

Seconds later Artemis entered the courtyard, gliding inches above its stone floor in silver-winged magic sandals. As Echo and the others watched, the goddessgirl searched the area with her keen dark eyes. Her bow was at the ready, and a quiver of silver arrows was slung across her back. "Come out, come out, wherever you are," she sing-songed under her breath as she zoomed around the fountain.

"See, she wants to meet us," murmured Narcissus, starting to stand.

"No, she's probably looking for that beast," Echo

whispered. She pointed toward the Drakon where it now stood in the shadows, its once-glowing red eyes now dull.

All forest nymphs were under Artemis's protection, and there was no goddessgirl they admired more. However, immortals mostly stayed up on Mount Olympus at the Academy, so Echo had only seen drawings of Artemis before now. Seeing her for real was *evergreen*! She took note of every one of the goddessgirl's mannerisms and her hairstyle, planning to copy her entire look when she got back . . . home. But where was that now? Unhappiness speared Echo anew.

"Artemis?" called a girl's voice from somewhere outside the maze.

Artemis glanced over her shoulder. "Over here! In the—" *Whap!* Not looking where she was going, she'd tripped over the Drakon. It seemed that the beast still had a few last sparks inside him after all, for some flew out as she went down.

Immediately Echo sprang out of the bushes. "Are you okay?"

"Huh? What happened?" Artemis shoved a lock of glossy black hair out of her eyes, looking dazed.

"You were attacked!" yelled Narcissus, jumping out of the bushes now too. "By him!"

Artemis noticed the beast for the first time. "Aha! I thought I heard a Drakon clanking around in here. This place is off-limits, you know. If the Pool of Magic is disturbed, it disturbs the mechanical beasts around here too. You guys are lucky *you* weren't all attacked. But that three-headed fountain there in the pool will turn any beast off including a Drakon, if I can just get over there." She pushed herself upright.

In a flash Narcissus was by her side and offering a

hand up. "No need!" he said gallantly. "I nailed that crazed beast myself. See? It's not moving."

Huh? Echo stared at him, surprised by his lie.

"Artemis, are you hurt? What's going on?" asked a new voice. Three immortal girls flew into the maze on winged sandals, one after the other.

Echo recognized Zeus's daughter, the brown-haired Athena, from her pictures, which were all over the news when she won various awards. And red-haired Persephone, too. The very goddessgirl whose clothes and hairstyle Echo had copied—and was wearing even now.

The third goddessgirl had long golden hair. She was so beautiful that she had to be Aphrodite. Like all immortals, the four girls' skin looked like it had been lightly powdered with glitter.

"I saved Artemis from a beast!" Narcissus announced,

fibbing again. "He started to attack her, and I knocked him down." He held up his spear in pretended victory.

Echo's eyes widened. Why was he lying like that?

"Well, thanks so much for rescuing her," Persephone said to Narcissus. Glancing around the group, she did a double take at the sight of Echo's chiton. Although she obviously noticed that it was a copy of the one she'd worn in the *Teen Scrollazine* drawing, she was kind enough not to mention the similarity.

"Yeah," Artemis began. "I really apprecia—"

"And my reward?" Narcissus asked eagerly.

Artemis blinked at him. "Excuse me?"

"Surely you'll grant me a favor for having rescued you," he prodded.

The four goddessgirls looked at each other as if uncertain how to respond. Finally, Artemis frowned at him. "You know, you remind me of someone. An actor I know." She glanced at her friends, who nodded in agreement.

Are they thinking of Orion? wondered Echo. Both boys were handsome. But although Narcissus did brag a bit (and tell a few harmless lies), she didn't think he was a total loser like Orion was rumored to be.

"Wow, thanks!" Narcissus said, obviously thinking Artemis had just paid him a compliment. "As it happens, I'm a model. So I was hoping for an introduction to Zeus. A powerful guy like him could boost my career."

"We do owe him," said Athena, glancing sideways at Narcissus.

Aphrodite nodded. "Yeah, you might have really been hurt without his help, Artemis."

"Zeus will want to thank him," Persephone added.

Still sounding somewhat reluctant, Artemis finally agreed. "Okay. Let's go in my chariot. It's faster than sandals, and we don't want to be late for next period."

"So you'll take me?" Narcissus pushed.

"And me, your assistant," Echo piped up boldly. Narcissus sent her a surprised look. But then he nodded, probably to keep her quiet about what had actually happened just minutes before!

"Me too," Tiresias added. "I'm his stylist."

"Yes," Narcissus agreed. "Oh, and my artist."

"Sorry. There's not enough room in the chariot," said Artemis. "We can only fit three of you."

"Well, at least my stylist," said Narcissus. "And . . ."

"Echo," said Echo, stepping forward and taking the choice out of his hands. This was *perfect*! It would take way less time to get to MOA in Artemis's chariot than on foot. The mortal artist Anaxandra looked crestfallen, and Echo felt kind of bad about that. But it seemed the girl lived in a nearby village, and when Tiresias promised they'd meet up with her later, she brightened and scampered off with her easel.

At Artemis's summons, four white deer with golden horns appeared out of the Forest and flew into the labyrinth, pulling her chariot behind them. "C'mon," she called to her companions. Jumping in, she took the reins, and Echo, Narcissus, and Tiresias crowded in with the goddessgirls. The chariot lifted off, and together they whooshed from the Forest.

5

Zeus

THE CHARIOT'S ASCENT WAS SWIFT, AND IN NO time it was zooming along as high as the treetops. Echo had never flown before and secretly held on tight, even as she copied the others' expressions of calm. Once she realized it was going to be smooth sailing, however, she relaxed for real and gazed excitedly at her surroundings.

Seeing her interest, the goddessgirls pointed out

landmarks below as they traveled, such as the Immortal Marketplace. It was a shopping center halfway up Mount Olympus, in an enormous, high-ceilinged building with a crystal roof.

"Interesting," said Narcissus, looking intrigued. "Are there clothes stores? Can mortals shop there?"

Athena nodded. "Yes. In fact, my dad's trying to encourage more mortal shoppers to come. Business has been a little slow ever since Typhon terrorized MOA. Storeowners have reported that shoppers are a little leery of leaving Earth to come to the IM."

Everyone had heard about Typhon, even nymphs like Echo in the forested mountains of Boeotia, Greece. He was a monster made of whirling tornado-strength winds that had escaped from imprisonment in Tartarus—the most awful place in the Underworld, where only the truly evil wound up. And he'd turned out to be evil, all right. He'd ravaged many lands before attacking Mount Olympus too.

"See those big decorated floats around the outside of the marketplace?" Aphrodite asked Echo. She pointed to a line of large colorful wheeled platforms that stretched halfway around the IM. "They're for tomorrow's parade."

Echo nodded, remembering the article in *Teen Scrollazine*. It would be fun to see the parade. But depending on what happened with Zeus this afternoon, she might or might not be in the mood to go tomorrow.

A little farther on, the goddessgirls also pointed out a snack shop called the Supernatural Market, where they sometimes hung out to sip nectar shakes. That certainly sounded like fun! As the chariot neared their final destination, they passed over sports fields and a gymnasium. Eventually the chariot landed in a marble-tiled courtyard in front of the Academy. There, Artemis's deer magically unhitched themselves and leaped away to graze in the nearby hills.

Echo gazed in wide-eyed wonder at the famous school. Built of polished white stone, it soared five stories high and was surrounded on all sides by Ionic columns. "Wow, I've never seen anything so awesome!"

"It's mega-mazing," Narcissus agreed, sounding awed. "This would make the perfect backdrop for a sketch of me, don't ya think?" He dashed across the courtyard and struck a pose next to a gadget that Athena informed them measured wind speed. The figures of the four wind gods had been sculpted on it. Their cheeks were puffed as if they were blowing out swirls of wind, and the instrument's main post was labeled *N, S, E,* and *W* for the different directions.

"With the Academy in the background, it would make an awesome shot," Tiresias agreed, squinting and framing Narcissus with his hands. "Too bad our artist couldn't come. We could've gotten some fashion drawings done for your portfolio that would have been far more impressive than those we tried to do in the Forest of the Beasts. Maybe we can scout locations for a future modeling session here, though."

"You'd have to ask my dad about that," Athena said tactfully. She and her friends led Narcissus, Tiresias, and Echo up the gleaming granite staircase at the front of the school.

Pushing through the bronze doors at the top of the stairs, the goddessgirls dropped their winged sandals into a big basket and slipped into regular sandals that they'd left there on the floor.

"Can we go see Zeus now? Who's going to take us?" asked Narcissus.

"I will," Artemis told her friends. "After all, I'm the one who almost got beaned by that Drakon this guy rescued me from." She arced a thumb in Narcissus's direction, and the other goddessgirls grinned at how bluntly she'd put things.

After the immortal girls parted company, Artemis turned down a hall and waved for Narcissus, Tiresias, and Echo to follow her. As they walked, Echo's eyes darted here and there. Everywhere she looked there was something or someone extraordinary to see. *Wait till I tell Daphne and Pan about all this!* she thought.

It was a huge thrill to recognize some of the students they passed. For instance, the mortal Medusa with a dozen green snakes on her head was easy to spot. And the guy with the trident was the godboy of the sea, Poseidon, of course. There was even a centaur!

Brightly colored paintings on the domed ceiling above the hallway detailed the glorious exploits of the gods and goddesses. One showed Zeus driving a chariot pulled by four white horses across the sky as he hurled thunderbolts and lightning into the clouds. *Hmph!* Didn't he know those bolts of his could be dangerous?

Echo's heart began to thump as she reminded herself of the main reason she'd come here. Her stomach had tightened into a pretzel knot by the time they moved down a final hallway and reached a door with a sign that read: OFFICE.

"Hello?" said Artemis, going inside. There was a

tall desk along one wall, but no one stood behind it. "Looks like Ms. Hydra's not here. She's Principal Zeus's administrative assistant," Artemis informed them. Passing the desk, she went to look into another office beyond it. The door of this one swung crazily from its one good hinge, creaking.

Narcissus and Tiresias followed Artemis, so Echo sidled over behind them and peeked in too. Her eyes practically bugged out at what she saw. This office was much bigger than the outer office. And it looked like a real tornado had swept through it!

File folders, scrolls, maps, pieces from an Olympusopoly board game, and empty bottles of Zeus Juice were scattered everywhere. Half-dead plants perched atop dented file cabinets, and chairs with scorch marks on their cushions sat tilted at odd angles. There was a huge golden throne behind the enormous desk on one side of the room. No one was sitting on it, though.

"Guess Principal Zeus is gone too," Artemis noted. "We'll have to come back later."

A mixture of disappointment and relief filled Echo. Then frustration set in. She'd been so close to realizing her goal of confronting Zeus about what he'd done to FirHeart!

Suddenly they heard footsteps, and then a dark-haired godboy raced into the office. When he saw Artemis, he blurted, "You okay, Sis? I heard you had an accident!"

"No big deal, Apollo," Artemis said easily. "Just a minor run-in with a Drakon Thespiakos."

"What?" said Apollo, his alarm increasing.

Narcissus stepped forward. "No worries. I saved her," he said smoothly. He went on to explain his version of what had happened. Afterward, Apollo thanked him sincerely.

Having heard these lies already, Echo decided it was much too late to correct his story. Besides, where was the harm, really? She glanced out the office window just in time to notice a winged horse take flight. That had to be Pegasus. And wasn't that Zeus on his back?

Hearing a swishing sound, she turned toward the front office door to see a lady with nine different-colored heads slither into the office.

"Hi, Ms. Hydra," said Artemis.

"Looking for Zeus?" the lady's smiling yellow head asked them in greeting. "He just left for the Immortal Marketplace."

"Come on. Let's go meet him there," Narcissus said to Artemis, starting for the door. Tiresias was right behind him.

"I don't think so. Artemis has a class," Ms. Hydra's purple head said in a disapproving tone. "And Zeus'll be busy. He's working on plans for the parade and a wedding. His guests of honor have arrived."

"Oh yeah. I saw something about that in *Teen Scrollazine*," said Echo. "There was a picture of him with two people who are going to get married and also with a goat and a bee."

"Those were his nannies—the goat and the bee, I mean," Ms. Hydra's yellow head told her. "They raised Zeus when he was a boy."

"The bride and groom who are getting married on Monday are nymphs too," Artemis told Echo. Then she looked over at Narcissus and said, "I guess we'll have to wait till Zeus gets back to tell him about your rescue. Apollo and I both need to start for class or we'll be late for sure."

"You can hang with me till Zeus comes back," Apollo told Narcissus and Tiresias as everyone left the office and started down the hall. "And you can meet the other guys at lunch." He smiled at Narcissus. "Heroes like you are welcome here!"

Argh, thought Echo as she and Artemis followed the boys. She was starting to wonder if she should have called Narcissus on his lie earlier. Could he have fooled himself into believing he really was a hero? No doubt he and Tiresias were already imagining how they could work that hero idea into drawings of Narcissus to add to his modeling portfolio.

"Fantastic!" Narcissus said to Apollo. "Contacts and networking are everything in my business."

"What business is that?" Apollo asked curiously as they all rounded a corner.

"Modeling," Echo heard Tiresias tell him. "Have you ever done any?"

Apollo jerked his head back in surprise. "Huh? Me, a model?"

"You're a natural," said Tiresias. "I should know. I've worked with the best."

"Meaning *me*," said Narcissus. Glancing over his shoulder at Echo, he dazzled her with another of his smiles.

She couldn't help smiling back. Modesty might not be his strong suit, but oh, how her heart sang whenever his attention turned her way!

"We hope to get some great portfolio shots here on the MOA grounds," Tiresias said to Apollo, confirming Echo's earlier suspicions. "We'd love to include you and your friends posing in the background paying tribute to Narcissus the hero."

Echo didn't hear Apollo's reply because Artemis said, "This way," and pulled her down a different hall. "You can come to my class and then hang out with me and my friends for the rest of the afternoon if you want," Artemis offered. "Don't ask me to do any modeling, though," she added with a grin.

Echo laughed. "No worries there. I don't know anything about that stuff. I'd only just met those mortals in the Forest when you showed up."

As they walked, her mind raced. Artemis was really nice to invite her to hang out, but Echo had other plans. She didn't want to wait for Zeus to get back. She wanted to talk to him now! The goddessgirls had pointed out the Immortal Marketplace as they'd flown here, and she figured she could probably find her way there on her own.

When they neared Artemis's classroom, Echo faked a yawn. "I'm kind of tired actually. What I could really use is a quick nap."

"Oh, well, you can go lie down in my dorm room," Artemis offered. She started to turn around. "I'll take you there."

"No, that's okay. I don't want to make you late. Just point the way," Echo urged. Artemis looked a little unsure, but after a bit more coaxing, she pointed up to the fourth-floor girls' dorm and indicated where her room was along the hall.

"My dogs are in my room, so be careful not to let them out," she cautioned. "There are three of them—Suez, Nectar, and Amby."

"Oh." Automatically, even though she had no intention of going up to Artemis's room, a shiver of fear ran down Echo's spine. She'd been chased by

93

hunting dogs out in the forest a few times. Artemis must have noticed the shiver, because she added quickly, "Don't worry. They're friendly."

"Great." Echo felt kind of guilty about tricking this nice goddessgirl, but she yawned again for good measure and assured Artemis that she could find the room. With a quick wave she started toward the stairs. But as soon as she was out of Artemis's sight, she changed direction.

After retracing her steps to the Academy's front door, she stopped beside the big basket there and glanced around. No one was looking. She reached into the basket to borrow a pair of winged sandals. She knew this had to be against the rules, but she was in a big fat hurry to track down the King of the Gods!

Quickly she headed out the front doors, down the school steps, and across the courtyard. At the far side of the marble expanse, she sat on a low stone bench. There she strapped the winged sandals on over her homemade vine ones, which were thin enough to fit inside the magic footwear. Immortals had the power to make these sandals fly, but would the wings work for a nymph, who only had half the magical power of a goddessgirl? Still seated, she unleashed the wings on the sandals. Big mistake.

The wings immediately started flapping, causing her feet to rise, so that her legs stuck straight out in front of her. The sandals tugged higher as if eager to fly, almost tipping her over backward.

"No! Wait. Stop," she called to them. If they took off now, she would fall backward on the bench and wind up flying upside down! Bending her knees to bring the sandals closer, she quickly leashed the wings again.

"I guess I should stand up before takeoff," she murmured, rising to her feet. "Let's try this again."

With both feet firmly on the ground, Echo braced one hand on a stone planter next to the bench. Then she reached down and unleashed the wings. As she straightened, the sandals lifted off to hover a few inches above the ground. *Success!*

Sort of. Back in the labyrinth the goddessgirls had made flying look effortless. Turned out it wasn't that easy. Her legs kept trying to do splits. And why wasn't she going anywhere? She pictured the way Artemis had looked when she'd flown into the maze that morning. Then she tried to do what the goddessgirl had done, straightening her legs, pressing them together, and then leaning forward a little. *Yes!* The sandals moved her ahead. And when she leaned back, they took her backward.

"Aha! I think I'm getting the hang of this," she murmured, zooming forward again. *Whack!* She bumped into a tree. "Notescroll to self, remember to bank left or right around solid objects," she mumbled. Leaning left now, she banked around the tree and winged off.

Although her nymph magic was enough to make the sandals fly, she found she wasn't able to achieve the same heights or speeds as the immortals. Still, an hour later she spotted the Immortal Marketplace, halfway down the mountain from MOA. She leaned back just a little, and her sandals began to slow. She touched down in front of the enormous, high-ceilinged building, then stumbled ahead a few steps before she was able to come to a complete stop.

After loosening the straps at her ankles, she looped them around the wings to hold them in place so she could walk normally. Straightening, she admired the colorful decorative floats she'd seen from Artemis's chariot that were outside the IM, being readied for the parade tomorrow. The air was filled with the sounds of saws and hammers and the smell of paint as workers busily added details to the floats, such as wooden figureheads and garlands of flowers. Should she check for Zeus out here? He might be overseeing the construction.

But then she heard another sound, a whinny. There, grazing behind one of the floats, was Zeus's white-winged horse, Pegasus. She went over and gave him a pat on the nose. "I bet you know where Zeus is, don't you?" Unfortunately, the horse couldn't talk and didn't reply.

Echo noticed, however, that Pegasus was standing near an outer door to the IM marked SHOP DELIVERY

ENTRANCE. Was Zeus beyond that door? She turned the knob and stepped into a delivery and storage area at the back of a shop. As she wound past racks of froufrou clothing to the main part of the shop, she heard what sounded like an interview in progress.

"Please tell us about your esteemed guests," a voice was asking someone she couldn't yet see.

"My pleasure," a booming voice replied. "As you all know by now, I grew up in a cave on Mount Ida in Crete. And Melissa and Amalthea were my nannies." This was Zeus speaking, of course. Heart thumping, Echo moved up to the edge of a crowd that had gathered to watch him being interviewed.

"Amalthea fed me goat milk and Melissa brought me honey," the seven-foot-tall King of the Gods went on. His muscles bulged, and electricity crackled off his arms as he gestured toward the goat beside him and a bee buzzing around his head. On cue the goat and bee shape-shifted into two women. Melissa (the bee nanny) had honey-colored hair and Amalthea (the goat nanny) had hair the color of milk.

"These ladies made me what I am today!" Zeus said, smiling at them broadly. "And now please meet Melissa's daughter, Ide, who is soon to be wed!" he proclaimed. A happy-looking younger woman with bee wings at her back stepped up to join the group, and Echo recognized her as the bride-to-be pictured in that article she'd seen in *Teen Scrollazine*. Her hair was honey-colored too, just like her mom's.

"My nannies are opening a shop right here in the Immortal Marketplace, with specialty soaps and candles with pure ingredients like beeswax and goats' milk," Zeus went on. "Tomorrow's parade will help showcase their products and the products of other IM stores too. Two dozen floats will circle outside the IM, tossing samples out to lucky shoppers in the parade crowds."

Breaking off momentarily, he posed for the reporter's artist, flexing his muscles and smiling big.

In the crowd near Echo, a man in a yellow-and-black checkered suit twirled his elaborate mustache, then leaned toward a woman with lots of skillfully applied makeup on her three eyes. "Good! The IM could use some promotion," he told her. The woman nodded, adding, "Too true. That Typhon windbag scared half of my Cleo's Cosmetics customers away, and they've never come back."

"The IM welcomes business from mortals, immortals, and everything in between. So pass it on," Zeus said, speaking now both to the reporter who'd been interviewing him and to the crowd. Abruptly, he paused, sniffing the air. A strange, dreamy look came over his face. "Well, thanks for listening, everyone! I have to go—King of the Gods business. I'll leave my nannies to take you on a tour of their store out in the IM. And don't forget—get out there and spread the word that the IM is safe and customers should come and START SHOPPING!"

Echo and those around her jumped at the loudness of Zeus's command. With the interview apparently over, the crowd began to spill out of the shop, along with his nannies. Everyone appeared to be heading into the main atrium of the marketplace, where Echo assumed most of the stores were located.

She ducked behind a rack of fancy chitons as Zeus said a hurried farewell to the reporter and ushered him out the door as well. Once they'd all gone, only the few workers who belonged in this shop remained. Zeus looked around as if to be certain the coast was clear. Then he made a beeline straight for a storage closet at the center of the shop. He pushed through the curtains that served as the closet's door and went inside.

Echo tiptoed over and paced outside the curtains for a few minutes. As she waited for Zeus to come out, she tried to work up the courage she would need to demand that he fix the problems he'd caused for her and her tree.

What was he up to in there, anyway? she wondered when he didn't come out right away. Could he be making new bolts of thunder and lightning? Plotting to strike something else with them just for fun? She was in the right, and he was in the wrong. What was she waiting for? It was now or never. She burst through the curtains.

6

Cupcakes

Zeus's back was to Echo, but he must have heard her enter the storage closet, because he whirled around at once. "Whah?" he mumbled. There was a guilty look on his face, as if he'd been caught stealing jewels. Actually, he was holding a cupcake and had a smear of pink frosting in his beard. She'd surprised him in the act of sneaking a snack!

For several seconds the two of them just stared

at one another. The gold thunderbolt on Zeus's belt buckle flashed, as did the gold bands at his wrists. Up this close, he towered over her like a giant.

Her feistiness had carried her this far, but suddenly Echo was feeling unsure. Confronting Zeus like this was a crazy idea. If she made him mad, he could zap her into smithereens in an instant.

But instead of zapping her, Zeus heaved a relieved sigh. "Oh gooh. Thought you wuh someone elsthe . . ." He finished off the pink cupcake he'd been holding and then popped a yellow one (lemon, maybe?) into his mouth, and finished in two bites. "Mmm," he said, sounding happy.

Echo frowned. Why should he get to be happy when he'd messed up her whole life? A renewed determination to make him pay filled her. "My name is Echo," she announced quickly, before she could change her mind. "I'm an Oreiad nymph, and you zapped my FirHeart with one of your lightning bolts!" Her voice trembled at her own daring.

"Whah? What's fur art? Art made out of fur?" Zeus replied around bites of a new cupcake. This one was dark brown, so probably chocolate.

"No, it's my tree!" she exclaimed. "I figured you were passing over the forested mountains of Boeotia the day before yesterday. Near the Forest of the Beasts?"

"Well, I . . . ," began Zeus, looking thoughtful.

"And one of your bolts struck my tree and destroyed it. Ka-boom!" She waved both hands outward to indicate a big explosion. Remembering the highly emotional moment, unhappiness welled up inside her.

Zeus swallowed the last bite of chocolate cupcake. "I was nowhere near the forest of Boeotia

Wednesday," he said, speaking clearly now. Then he pulled a strawberry off a fresh cupcake. Echo noticed there was a whole platter of various flavored ones on the counter behind him. Zeus popped the strawberry into his mouth and then gobbled the cupcake. He offered her one, but she shook her head. How could he eat at a time like this?

"What? But you must have been," she insisted. "There was lightning. And a bolt struck my tree!" She thrust her chin forward. "And so I want you to . . . No, I demand that you . . ."

At her forceful tone Zeus frowned. Electricity sizzled up and down his mighty arms. *Uh-oh.* She'd better be careful. She'd heard what could happen if someone made him mad. And she'd seen those scorch marks in his office. She took a step back, hoping he wasn't planning to zap her.

But before he could speak or act, a woman's voice called to him from outside the closet's curtains.

"Zeus?"

At the sound of that voice, Zeus's eyes practically boinged out of their sockets. Now he was the one who looked scared. With his big hands holding three more cupcakes, and with icing in his beard, he looked like a little kid caught breaking a no-sweets rule.

"Zeus?" the woman called through the curtains again. "Are you in there?"

Echo watched him toss the three cupcakes he'd been holding over his shoulder to land back on the platter. *Plop! Plop! Plop!* His blue eyes blazed into Echo's brown ones. "I'll give you anything you want if you stall her," he hissed.

"Stall her?" Echo repeated, not understanding. "Stall who?"

"Hera! My wife! She owns this shop." Without waiting for a reply, Zeus put a hand on Echo's back and pushed her out through the slit in the curtains.

"Eek!" she squeaked. He probably hadn't meant to, but he'd zapped her a little. Echo lurched out of the storage closet and came face-to-face with the regal-looking Hera. She had thick blond hair styled high up on her head, and a no-nonsense look in her eye. Although she wasn't unusually tall, she was statuesque.

"Oh, hello, young lady," Zeus's wife said, looking at her with a mix of surprise and curiosity.

"Oh, hello," Echo repeated, trying to get Hera's accent just right. She felt an instant desire to copy the goddess's voice. It was so beautiful, melodious, and full of confidence.

"What were you doing in the . . ." the woman

started to say, glancing at the curtain behind Echo.

Zeus had promised to give Echo anything she wanted. So, hoping that it might be within his power to restore FirHeart to life, she began to chatter non-stop, trying to draw Hera away from the curtained storage room as Zeus had requested.

"I'm Echo," she said cheerily. "This bakery is sooo mega-cool. Is it yours? I mean, you don't really look like a chef or anything. And this doesn't exactly look like a bakery, but—"

"Oh, well, it's not . . ." the woman began.

"Really?" Echo interrupted. She gestured toward a table of delicacies near the front of the shop and started to move in that direction, hoping Hera would follow. "Then what's all this yummy-looking stuff?" she said as she went past more racks of clothing toward the table. "Cakes, pillow mints, heart-shaped cookies, candies, macaroons, chocolates. Oh, maybe this is a sweets shop? But then what are all the racks of frilly clothes for?"

Unfortunately, Hera stayed where she was. "The foods are samples. So are the chitons," said the shop goddess, craning her neck toward the curtained storage area as if she suspected what Echo was up to. "This is a wedding shop."

Echo hurried back to block the curtain. "It is? Wow! No wonder everything looks so dreamy and extra special."

"Well, my shop does specialize in happy endings," said Hera. She stepped to one side of Echo as if she meant to go around her and push through the curtain.

"Oh!" Echo took a step in the same direction, blocking the goddess again. She clasped her hands

111

together in excitement that, though exaggerated, was genuine. "I've heard of your shop! Hera's Happy Endings, right?" Taking a good look around the store, she saw that it contained much more than bridal chitons. There were shelves with long gloves and sandals dyed to match, as well as tiaras and books with ideas for invitations, flower arrangements, and bridal gown adornments. For someone with an interest in fashion like her, this shop was *better* than a sweets shop!

"Exactly. Brides try these sample wedding chitons on and choose one, and then we create an identical but completely new chiton for them, using their measurements. Sometimes the bride makes a few alterations in the design, and we always add embellishments—"

"Like for the wedding I read about in *Teen Scrollazine*? Is the chiton for that bride in here? Could I see it?"

"No. It has already shipped out," Hera said in exasperation. "Now, young lady, could you please stop talking and—" But Echo's words were like a runaway chariot. She jabbered on and on, mostly from interest, but also hoping to give Zeus time to escape or hide the evidence or whatever. What was he doing in there anyway?

At last, just as Echo ran out of things to say, the curtains behind her parted and Zeus stepped from the storage closet to join them. "Well, hello, sugarplum," he said to Hera, bending to give her a peck on the cheek.

Hera folded her arms and gazed at him with suspicion. "What were you doing in there with those cupcakes?"

"Cupcakes?" Zeus echoed innocently.

Echo grinned. Ha-ha. Even the King of the Gods

113

repeated what people said now and then. It was a good stalling tactic, if nothing else.

"The *sample* cupcakes," said Hera. She whipped the curtains open and stepped into the storage closet. Echo peeked in too, and gasped. All the cupcakes were gone! There must've been about two dozen of them on those platters. Had Zeus eaten them all?

"That's odd. The Oracle-O Bakery was supposed to put samples in here so that Ide could taste them and choose which she liked best before her wedding on Monday," said Hera. "I wonder what happened to my order?"

Was that really what Zeus was doing while I was talking to Hera? Echo thought in amazement. Finishing off a couple dozen cupcakes? All by himself? Then she noticed a drop of pink icing on his tunic. While

Hera's back was turned, Echo pointed to it, whispering, "Icing."

Zeus's brows scrunched together, indicating that he hadn't understood. He sent her a questioning look just as Hera turned back. His wife caught the look, and the suspicion in her eyes increased.

Hera frowned at Echo, as if sure that she was in cahoots with Zeus and they were playing some trick. Then Hera's eyes dropped to the pink spot on Zeus's chest. "Is that icing on your tunic?"

"Uh," said Zeus, quickly wiping at the spot. "Must be that honey Melissa sent. I gave it a tiny taste so the *Greekly Weekly* artist could draw me enjoying it, remember?"

Hera wagged a finger at him. "*Pink* honey? I don't think so, mister."

Echo thought fast. "Wait!" she exclaimed. "Please

don't be mad. It was me. I ate most of the cupcakes. Zeus was just covering for me," she fibbed. "You see, er, I'm going to be a bridesmaid in a wedding soon, and the bride-to-be asked me to scout around for ideas. I came a long way from the forest and was starving by the time I got here." She wasn't sure where the words came from, but they did the trick. Hera's attention was caught.

"Oh? A wedding? Like I was saying before, if there's one thing I know about, it's weddings," said Hera. "Invitations, flowers, fancy chitons for special occasions . . ."

Bam! Just then the main shop door blew open and a scroll flew in on a honey-scented breeze. It went straight to Hera. After unrolling the scroll and scanning its message, she looked a little exasperated.

"Problem?" Zeus asked. "Can I help?"

Hera looked up and blinked at him, quickly closing the scroll as the breeze blew away. "Oh. No. No problem at all," she replied in a perky voice. But her smile was a little strained and didn't quite reach her eyes, Echo noticed. "Ide was just in the store and said the bridal chiton we designed for her was perfect. However, she has apparently changed her mind in the last few minutes and will be returning it today with a request for some changes," Hera explained. "Nothing I can't handle."

"Well, she's in good hands. With you in charge, hers is sure to be the wedding of the century!" Zeus seemed to be trying extra hard to be nice to his wife after the cupcake caper.

Hera smiled fondly at him. "I know how much Melissa means to you, and that makes her daughter's wedding super important to me. I'm happy to help in any way I can."

Then her expression firmed, and she gestured toward the empty cupcake platters in the closet, which Zeus had failed to hide. "But I'm still a little disappointed in you. Echo may have eaten some of these cupcakes, but I have a feeling you helped. We talked about this sort of binging on sweets. Are you going to cut back and start eating healthfully?"

"Sure, anything you say, honeybun," Zeus soothed. "Mmm. Honeybuns," he murmured blissfully.

Echo stared at him, astonished. He'd just killed off two dozen cupcakes and was still drooling for snacks? Apparently the King of the Gods had a major sweet tooth!

Even Hera had to laugh at that, though she quickly grew serious again. "You promised to work on your diet," she scolded. "And I promised to create the perfect wedding for Melissa's daughter. I'm keeping my end of our bargain. You need to summon up the willpower to keep yours."

Zeus straightened, looking slightly affronted. "I'm a god of my word. And a willpower king. Why, I could go years without sweets. Well, maybe months. Well, make that weeks."

"Then prove it," said Hera. "How about *one* week? No sugary sweets for one whole week."

"But what about the wedding on Monday?" Zeus protested, gazing longingly toward the samples on the sweets-laden table behind her.

"Exactly. What better time to show all those who come to the wedding that you are a man of healthy eating habits and unshakable willpower? Everyone looks up to you. Set a good example for them."

"Okay," he mumbled, sounding down in the dumps.

At the sound of a doorbell tinkling, someone came into the store and Hera turned to go. Then she glanced back at Echo, adding, "Tell your friend who's getting married to come by the shop. Anytime after Monday, when we won't be so busy. I'll be delighted to help her create the perfect wedding."

Echo nodded. Hera was so nice that she felt kind of bad that she didn't actually know any brides-to-be. She'd keep her eyes and ears open, though, and send any she heard about in future to this awesome shop.

After Hera left, Zeus seemed to forget all about Echo and headed off toward the delivery exit, where Pegasus awaited him.

She caught up to him just before he left the store. "Wait! You said you're a god of your word. And you

120

promised me anything I asked for if I helped stall Hera. And I did, so . . ."

Zeus nodded, looking thoughtful. "Yes, you did. Tell you what, I can't mend your tree, but I have another idea that might help you."

"No!" Echo exclaimed, before he had even told her his idea. "You messed things up, and now I want you to fix FirHeart!"

Zeus folded his arms and tapped his big gold-sandaled foot impatiently. "Sorry, but I didn't have anything to do with that lightning bolt that struck your tree, no matter what you think. And bringing your tree back to life or giving you a new one would be against the rules. Rules I made. Still, since you helped me, I think I can bend—"

"Yes?" Echo interrupted eagerly, her eyes brightening with new hope.

"A different rule," Zeus finished. "One that will allow you to move to another realm and become a different kind of nymph."

"But FirHeart—" protested Echo.

"Not gonna happen," he informed her, slicing a big meaty hand through the air. "That rule can't be bent. Maybe the forest isn't right for you. The job of protecting one specific tree is a lot of responsibility. On the other hand, nymphs in non-forest realms *share* responsibility. They band together as a team to protect an entire river, or a bunch of clouds." His intense blue eyes looked into her brown ones. "My offer's a good one," he said in a firm but not unkind voice. "Take it. Choose another realm where you'll be more of a team player. I'll give you a week to decide where you want to relocate. Okay?"

Suddenly there was a rustling movement in one of

the racks of clothes next to Zeus. To Echo's surprise, Athena peeked out at her from between two chitons on hangers where Zeus couldn't see her.

Say, yes! the goddessgirl mouthed silently. Then Aphrodite's head popped out next to Athena's and nodded emphatically. And two hands shot out a little farther down the rack, each giving Athena's suggestion a thumbs-up.

"Yes, okay," Echo told Zeus. But she wasn't happy about it.

7

Choices

AFTER ZEUS EXITED THE WEDDING SHOP, ATHENA, Aphrodite, Persephone, and Artemis sprang out of the rack of chitons. Shushing Echo, they quickly and quietly ushered her out of the shop into the atrium, careful not to alert Hera or her employees to their presence.

"Sorry for all the sneaking around back there,"

Aphrodite told Echo as the five of them strolled in the general direction of the IM exit.

Echo hardly noticed the shops they passed. Filled with hopelessness, it didn't even occur to her to ask what the girls had been doing, hiding out at Hera's. All she could think about was one horrible fact: It looked like FirHeart was really and truly gone forever.

"We didn't want Zeus to know we skipped class to come here," Persephone explained, though Echo hadn't asked. "We *had* to come because we were concerned about your safety!"

"Yeah," said Artemis. "I saw your wild takeoff in those winged sandals through a school window. So I grabbed these three guys from class to help me track you down and make sure you were okay."

"How long were you in the shop?" Echo asked. Just how much had they seen and heard of her conversations with Zeus and Hera?

"A few minutes," Athena said. "It took us a while to find you. We sneaked in behind that customer Hera was with just now."

"We heard what Zeus told you, though," Persephone said in a gentle voice. "I'm so sorry about your tree. I get upset when even one of my flowers dies, so I can imagine how truly awful you must feel." Her friends nodded, their expressions sympathetic.

"Yeah," Echo said sadly.

"We're all sorry," Athena assured her. "But if my dad had been responsible for what happened to your tree, I know he wouldn't lie about it."

Echo thought back to the FirHeart disaster. It was true that she hadn't actually heard thunder that day, and Zeus's lightning and thunder usually went together. The *ka-boom* had been the sound of her tree splitting. However, if Zeus hadn't caused her tree to split, then who had?

"So are you going to give Principal Zeus's idea a chance and switch to a different realm?" Aphrodite asked.

Echo shrugged and let out a heavy sigh. "Yeah, I guess." What choice did she have? A panicked feeling filled her at the thought of having to reset the course of her life. "I don't know what realm to choose, though."

Just then they passed a store called the Oracle-O Bakery and Scrollbooks. "You know what we need to jump-start this decision of yours? Snacks," said Artemis, glancing pointedly toward the shop.

"Good idea. Seeing all that yummy wedding food

in Hera's shop made me hungry. Plus we're missing lunch. Let's grab some snacks to go," suggested Athena.

Did this girl share the same sweet tooth as her dad? Echo wondered. But then she got a whiff of the heavenly smell of cookies herself and caved instantly. "Mmm. I guess one won't hurt." She reached for the door.

Inside the shop they found Artemis's brother, Apollo, chatting with a girl with fire-gold hair who was wearing sun-and-moon earrings. "Hey, skipping class?" Apollo teased, raising his brows at the girls.

"I might ask you the same," said Artemis. As Athena, Aphrodite, and Persephone began browsing the store, the girl Apollo had been chatting with moved to help them.

"I have an excuse. An official one," Apollo told

Artemis, waving a small MOA scrollpass under her nose. "My band is playing in the parade tomorrow. So I left Narcissus with some of the guys, and I'm here getting everything set up."

"We have an excuse too. We're seeing to the safety of a visitor from another realm, who had a meeting with Zeus," Artemis replied, fudging the truth a little. "Echo, you already met my brother, Apollo. And that's Cassandra." She motioned to the girl he'd been talking to.

The fire-gold-hair girl smiled and waved from across the store, where she was now recommending various cookies to the other goddessgirls. "Nice to meet you!"

As Apollo munched a cookie he'd already half-finished, Echo and Artemis wandered over to make their selections. "There are so many choices,"

Persephone was saying, pondering the snacks.

Tell me about it, thought Echo. If they thought it was hard choosing cookies, they should imagine how hard choosing a whole new path for your life would be.

"I'm going for a Mount Olympus Mint Crunch. What are you guys going to get?" asked Aphrodite.

"Ooh! That sounds good. I'll have one of those too," said Echo. But every time someone else made a choice of cookie, it sounded so good that she changed her order to the new flavor. She just couldn't help copying!

After a while Athena sent her a perplexed glance and suggested, "Let's just get an assortment to share."

As they checked out, Echo found herself standing next to Apollo. The front of his tunic had a logo for a band called Heavens Above. Oh yeah! That was the group Pan was longing to play with.

"Do you ever add new band members?" she blurted out. "I have this friend named Pan. He's an amazing musician."

"Well, sometimes we need a sub on an instrument, but to join the band on a regular basis we'd require a true talent with a rare sound," said Apollo. "Tell you what, though. Your friend can come by our bandstand outside the IM's main entrance tomorrow after the parade if he wants to meet me and the guys."

Pan would be disappointed to hear there were no openings in the band, but he'd be thrilled at Apollo's invitation to meet the band's members. Echo wasn't sure he was up to the level of those performers. Still, she hoped he was good enough to be given an opportunity to at least jam with them if he showed up with an instrument. He'd be heartbroken if they refused him.

"Thanks," she told Apollo. "Though I'm not sure how I'll get word to him, since I . . . uh . . . might not be returning to the forest for a while." Or *ever*, she thought, remembering the choice she was going to have to make.

"No problem," said Athena, overhearing. "We can buy a blank wingscroll in the scrollbooks side of this shop. You can write him a message and fly it to him."

After a brief hesitation Echo nodded. "Good plan, thanks." After all, in addition to sending Apollo's invitation, she should let Pan and Daphne know what was going on with her. They'd worry if they didn't hear.

Athena quickly got her a scroll, and Echo wrote a note. Minutes later the small determined scroll winged away, carrying her message to Pan, who would share Echo's news with Daphne.

Soon afterward Echo and the four goddessgirls

left the shop together. As they munched their cookies and window-shopped, they also chatted about the
various store displays.

Echo reached into the bag without looking and
let fate decide her choice. She pulled out a Vanilla
Thrilla cookie and took a bite.

"You will seek advice when it's needed," said a
small voice.

Echo looked around, her eyes wide. "Who said that?"

"It's your cookie. Each Oracle-O speaks a fortune
when you take a bite," said Persephone, giggling. She
bit into hers.

"You will ride the waves," it told her.

"True!" Persephone said. "I'll be on Poseidon's float
tomorrow in the parade. It's got a sea theme. Naturally."

The other three goddessgirls grinned at that,
but Echo turned serious. "Mine's right too. I could

really use some advice. Can you guys help me? I mean, there are so many kinds of nymphs. What kind do you think I should be?" She looked at the four goddessgirls. They sent each other uncertain glances, seeming reluctant to make suggestions.

"I don't think we can really weigh in until we know more about you," Athena remarked at last.

Echo shrugged. "What do you want to know?"

"Well, how about if we start with your style?" prompted Aphrodite. She gestured toward the window of a shop they were passing called the Green Scene, where all the clothes on display were in shades of green. "When I have to make a decision, sometimes I think of it in terms of fashion. Do I want frilly, elegant, simple, athletic, outdoorsy?"

"I never knew that about you," said Persephone, teasing her in a friendly way.

"You let clothes decide things for you?" Artemis asked at the same time. She sounded aghast. "What happens if your cloak and your chiton don't agree?"

Everyone laughed.

Afterward, Artemis's expression turned thoughtful. "It so happens that I know most of the nymphs in Greece. So why don't we all go visit various realms to check them out?"

"Good plan!" said Athena.

"Yeah. It'll be like trying the realms on to see if they suit you," Aphrodite told Echo with a teasing glance toward Artemis. "Sort of like trying on a new chiton to see if it fits and looks good."

Artemis rolled her eyes at the clothing comparison, but Persephone high-fived Aphrodite and shouted, "Yes!"

These goddessgirls seem a lot more excited about this

whole idea than I am, thought Echo. Maybe that was a good thing. Someone had to make her do this. And these nice, fun girls were on a mission to help her. So she'd let them!

The minute all five girls burst out of the IM, they released the wings on their sandals. The goddess-girls lifted off and began moving ten times the speed of walking as they rose ever higher. When Athena noticed that Echo was struggling to keep up, she darted back down and offered a hand. "Grab on."

Echo did, and found herself pulled upward to heights only immortals could achieve. "But where should we go first?" she asked as they flew off in a group.

"I think there's a meadow up ahead," said Artemis. "Those are usually full of Leimonide nymphs, so what do you say?"

Echo took a fortifying breath. "Okay, let's do it."

"Great! Let's go!" Artemis cheered. Moving slightly ahead, she guided them all to a meadow covered with lavender, yellow, pink, and white wildflowers.

"Where is everybody?" asked Aphrodite, glancing around after they touched down in the peaceful meadow. It was heart-shaped and was bordered by large, lush green hills.

"You'll see," said Artemis. She let out a series of gentle whistles.

Suddenly nymphs that had been unnoticeable before sprang up from the tall grass. Since their skin was the same green color as the meadow, and their chitons and hair were dotted with wildflowers, they'd blended in.

The Leimonide nymphs flitted forward and looped daisy chain necklaces around the five girls'

necks. Slender hands reached out to them.

"Come join our dance!" coaxed one of the nymphs, swooping and twirling around the girls.

"Yes, do!" trilled another. She whirled in a circle, while others did cartwheels and beckoned their guests deeper into the meadow.

"I'm coming!" shouted Artemis, running after the nymphs. Aphrodite, Athena, and Persephone laughed, allowing themselves to be whisked away to frolic across the meadow too.

After a brief hesitation, Echo joined in, shouting, "Wait for me!" Her last word bounced back to her ears from the surrounding hills. *Me-ee-ee!*

"Faster! Faster! Dance!" the nymphs urged, pulling the girls along. And dance the five visitors did, unable to stop, no matter how weary they became. Somewhere in the grass a musical stream bubbled, playing music to which they all pirouetted, romped, and skipped.

"I'm so tired!" Aphrodite called at last to Echo and the others. "But I can't seem to stop!"

"Me either!" Athena replied breathlessly.

"It's impossible!" Echo agreed, twirling in circles like a mini tornado.

"I wonder if it's these daisy necklaces that make us keep dancing," said Persephone.

"Take them off!" said Artemis, flinging hers away immediately.

The other four girls yanked off their necklaces too. And at last they were able to stop dancing. Still the meadow nymphs pulled on their hands, reluctant to lose their new playmates. But when the exhausted girls refused to budge, the nymphs left them behind and merrily continued on their way across the meadow.

After the nymphs were gone, Echo and the four

goddessgirls plopped down onto the grass and stared at each other, their chests heaving.

"Well, that was fun. Sort of. But I don't think it's for me," Echo said, finally.

"No?" said Athena, laughing. "I can't imagine why." She stretched out on her back among the flowers, and the others did the same, relaxing and trying to catch their breath.

"What now?" asked Persephone after they'd rested a few minutes.

Aphrodite gazed upward, as if deep in thought. "Hey! I know," she said suddenly. "See those clouds? You could become a Nephelai!" Those were nymphs that dwelled within rain clouds.

"Hmm," Echo said uncertainly.

"C'mon, just give it a try. You never know, right?" Athena grabbed one of Echo's hands, and Artemis took the other. Together they whisked her high into the clouds that ringed Mount Olympus, while Aphrodite and Persephone followed.

Eventually they came upon a dozen nymphs with pearly white skin and long locks of hair that resembled newly picked cotton. Some were doing flips and somersaults in the clouds. Others were playing easy games like hide-and-seek or ring-around-the-rosy. All seemed to be giggling nonstop.

"Elcome-wizzle!" a nymph greeted them in the language of the Nephelai. Her breath came out in frosty white puffs.

"Ank-thizzle ou-yizzle!" Artemis replied. Then to Echo and the others, she confided, "When they aren't telling jokes, they speak Drizzle Latin. It's like pig latin, only you add "izzle" and "yizzle" instead of "ay" and "yay.""

"Oh-yizzle, I-yizzle et-gizzle it-yizzle," said Athena. Which of course meant "Oh, I get it."

Hearing Athena speak their language, the nymphs giggled so hard that some of them got the hiccups.

"Do they always giggle this much?" Echo whispered doubtfully.

Artemis nodded. "Their funny, bubbly personalities are what keep them aloft in the rain clouds."

Within seconds the five visitors found themselves giggling too, because giggles were catching. And when they weren't speaking in Drizzle, these cloud nymphs were constantly telling jokes, which they quickly answered themselves!

"What happens when it rains cats and dogs?" said one. "You might step in a poodle."

"How does a bee keep dry in the rain?" asked another nymph. "With a yellow jacket."

"How can you gift wrap a cloud?" asked yet another nymph. "With a rainbow."

As silly as the jokes were, they still caused Echo and the goddessgirls to laugh. And suddenly Echo found herself copying the Nephelai and contributing her own silly jokes. "What did one raindrop say to another?" she asked. "Two's company, three's a cloud." Which cracked them all up anew.

The four goddessgirls seemed to catch the joke-telling bug too. "What falls but never gets hurt?" Persephone asked. "Rain."

All the giggling, joking, and somersaulting in the clouds was really fun. However, it turned out that this was pretty much the only thing cloud nymphs *did* all day. They seemed to be as fluffy and lightweight as clouds themselves—in the brain department!

After motioning the other girls aside so that the

Nephelai wouldn't overhear, Aphrodite asked, "What did one goddessgirl say to her friends?" Then she answered her own joke. "Get me outta here!"

"Yeah, these airheads are not at all down to Earth," Echo added, which sent them all into giggles again.

"Earth. Hmm. That gives me an idea," said Persephone as the girls bid the Nephelai good-bye and whisked down from the clouds. "How about trying the Lampiades next?"

"Nymphs of the Underworld? The ones that dwell *below* the Earth?" Athena asked as they flew aimlessly onward for the moment.

Echo's alarm must've shown on her face. "The Underworld? I don't think that's for me. Isn't it where that awful place Tartarus is?"

"Everyone always thinks of Tartarus first, but there's much more to the Underworld," Persephone told Echo. "In fact, if I put in a good word, I'm sure Hades would let you into the Elysian Fields. It's mega-awesome. The happiest place below Earth! Are you sure you don't want to go see what it's like there?"

"Well . . . ," Echo began. She wished she could find a way to say no to this idea without hurting Persephone's feelings.

"I'm with Echo on this one. Just thinking about the Underworld makes me feel hot and gloomy," said Artemis.

"Then let's go cool off. Anyone for a nice dip in a cool river?" suggested Aphrodite.

Hands went up.

"Okay," said Persephone, grinning. "I can take a hint. No Underworld."

The five girls dipped lower, studying the landscape below as they flew on. Ten minutes later they spotted a rocky gorge with colorful vegetation growing up its steep sides. A river rushed through its depths like a sparkling jeweled ribbon of blue. And from it sprang Naiads laughing and flowing along with the current. Unlike Syrinx, these river nymphs seemed nice.

"Come on in!" they called to Echo and the goddessgirls. "The water's great!"

"Wait, first let me do a spell that'll make sure we come out of this river as dry as we went in. Wouldn't want to return to MOA looking like wet sponges," said Aphrodite. Then she chanted:

> *"How dry we are,*
> *How dry we'll be,*
> *When we return*
> *From our swimming spree!"*

"Woo-hoo! Let's go with the flow!" Artemis shouted once the spell was complete. She did a cannonball into the river. *Splash!* One by one Echo and the other three goddessgirls dropped into the river after her. *Splash! Splash! Splash! Splash!*

Echo soon found herself floating along through frothing water with the goddessgirls and the nymphs. The water's gentle force pulled them under arched bridges and past fantastic crystal-clear waterfalls flowing from steep rocks on the high sides of the gorge. From there they floated on past fir-tree-covered mountains with ancient temples on high bluffs.

Together the goddessgirls and nymphs swam and splashed each other. Occasionally a few of them got out of the water to dive from a rock. Echo corkscrewed, freestyled, and backstroked. The buoyant water seemed to wash away her cares, and she found she was happy just to bob along with the current, never questioning where it was taking her. She could get used to this. No wonder Daphne sometimes missed the river!

Suddenly the calm, easygoing river nymphs began talking in a rush. "Squeee!" "Yahoo!" "White water downstream. Look out for the undertow!"

"Ye gods! Abandon the river! We're headed for wild rapids and a waterfall dead ahead!" yelled Artemis. She grabbed Echo's hand mere seconds before they would have been swept over the falls. They swam to safety alongside Aphrodite, Persephone, and Athena.

Phew! thought Echo, glad to have escaped the fall. Fortunately, Aphrodite's spell had worked, and when they all climbed out onto the riverbank, they were dry.

Together the five girls zoomed into the air and hovered above the river momentarily, waving to the Naiads and watching them go over the falls one by one. Emerging unscathed at the bottom, the river nymphs swam merrily onward through the gorge.

"Wow! Those Naiads are daredevils!" said Echo. "Their river was fun for a while, but I'm used to the forest. Things happen more slowly there." Then, worried that these goddessgirls might think her ungrateful, she added, "Not that I can't change. If I have to."

"You shouldn't commit to a lifestyle you don't want, though," Aphrodite advised, turning to wing back to the Academy now.

"Yeah. Zeus is bending the rules and is unlikely to do it twice. Once you make a choice, there's no going back," warned Artemis as she and the others followed.

"So be sure to choose a realm you really like," said Athena, flying backward to talk to Echo, who was flying alongside Persephone.

Persephone looked sideways at Echo, "You have a lot to think about, yes?"

"Yes," Echo repeated. "But I really appreciate you guys showing me my options." She put on a smile to thank them for their kindness. Inside she was all fluttery worry, though. Those places had been fun to visit, but she wouldn't want to live in any of them. Yet without a tree of her own, she didn't fit in to the mountain forests anymore either.

So what was she going to do?

8

Copycat

"READY TO TALK TO MY DAD?" ATHENA ASKED Echo as the girls landed in MOA's courtyard a short time later. There were just four of them now—Athena, Aphrodite, Artemis, and Echo. Persephone lived off campus with her mom and had parted from them to head home after they'd left the river.

"Not yet," said Echo as they all pushed through the bronze doors into the Academy and began trading their winged sandals for their normal ones. "I need to think some more."

Aphrodite nodded. "You'll know the right choice when you feel it in your heart."

"You should sleep on it," Artemis advised. "Like I said before, you can spend the night in my room, if you want. I don't have a roommate, so I've got a spare bed." Then she added, "And if you want to try some other nymph realms next week, I'm game."

"Thanks. I'll think about it," Echo told her with real gratitude. At least she had a temporary home and some hope for the future.

"How about some food for thought?" Aphrodite suggested. "I say we hit the cafeteria for dinner."

"Good idea," said Athena. "After all that dancing, cloud-tumbling, and swimming, I'm starving again!"

Once inside the cafeteria, the four girls grabbed

trays and went through the dinner line. An eight-armed lady served up helpings of ambrosia salad and something called nectaroni. Then Echo's new friends invited her to eat at their table in the dining area. After she sat down, she took in the scene around her.

Over at a nearby table she saw Medusa, Pandora, Pheme, and another girl she didn't recognize. Medusa was tossing small objects that looked like peas and pieces of carrot into the air around her head, and her snakes were snapping them up!

Echo took a sip of the nectar the goddessgirls were drinking, wondering if it would make her skin glitter like theirs. No such luck. She looked over at the mortals, Pandora and Medusa, and saw that the nectar was having no effect on them, either.

Apollo was back from the IM, she noticed. Narcissus and Tiresias were sitting with him and his godboy friends. She recognized Ares, Poseidon, Hades, and Heracles among them. Wow! It was hard to believe she was hanging out with all these wildly popular immortals. If only Daphne and Pan could be here too.

Apollo's friends had finished eating already. Now, after pushing two tables together, they were entertaining everyone around them by building towers of leftovers atop their lunch trays and seeing who could carry theirs the most times around their tables before their tower collapsed.

A bunch of giggly girls at an adjacent table were rooting for Narcissus to win. Who could blame them? He was fantastically cute and also proving to be a good athlete! The girls clapped after he made it around the tables five times. Then he posed, holding his tray on the flat of one hand. When his blue eyes flicked to Echo, she quickly looked away, a little embarrassed to be caught staring.

Noticing the direction of Echo's gaze, Aphrodite smiled at her. "So, is Narcissus a special friend of yours?" the goddessgirl asked casually as she stacked empty dishes onto her tray.

"Better watch it. Aphrodite is the goddessgirl of love, you know," Athena teased Echo. "She's always trying to make matches."

Echo took a sip of nectar, feeling her cheeks turn as red as an autumn leaf. "No, he's not my crush or anything. Like I told Artemis, I met him just before I met you guys. And he seems to have more than enough admirers already." She glanced over to see that those giggly girls were now at the godboys' table, talking to him.

"Only trying to help," Aphrodite said gently. "I enjoy guiding friends toward happiness."

"Are you saying Narcissus and I might be good together?" Echo asked eagerly.

"Possibly. But I'm not yet sure of . . ." Aphrodite started to say.

"What's been up, Echo? Where have you guys been?" a voice suddenly interrupted.

Echo whipped around to see that Narcissus had come over. Surprised by his sudden arrival, she fumbled around for a reply. The three goddessgirls bailed her out by saying they'd simply gone exploring.

Then Aphrodite stood up with her tray. "We'd better get moving, goddessgirls. We've got that, um, stuff to go do," she said with a meaningful glance in Artemis's and Athena's direction.

"What stuff? I wasn't finished eating," Artemis began, totally missing the hint.

Athena elbowed her and stood too. "C'mon. We

156

should save room for snacks later, Artemis. It's Friday night, after all. And, um, we had plans to go to the Supernatural Market later, remember?"

"No, but okay," Artemis said reluctantly. Then she looked at Echo. "Coming?"

"You can meet us in the dorm hall later," Aphrodite quickly told Echo. Then the three girls headed off to the tray return, leaving Echo with Narcissus.

Echo's heart beat fast. Were those goddessgirls purposely trying to give the two of them a chance to talk because they thought Narcissus might be starting to crush on her? He hadn't seemed to even notice her in the cafeteria till now, but he *had* broken away from his admirers at last and singled her out.

"So you and those immortals are friends now?" Narcissus asked, nodding after the three departing

157

goddessgirls. "They're the most popular girls at this school. Good work."

"Work?" Echo repeated, standing with her tray. He made it sound like she'd purposely set out to make friends with Aphrodite, Athena, and Artemis. And it hadn't been like that at all. If anything, *they'd* befriended *her*. "They were just helping me with a problem," she said. "See, Zeus told me to—"

"You met *Zeus*? The big guy himself?" Narcissus interrupted, sounding impressed. "Did you tell him about me?"

"Well, no. You didn't come up," said Echo, surprised.

At this news Narcissus wilted like a flower denied water and sunlight. As he followed her to the tray return, Echo tried to explain. "I'm sorry I didn't mention you. I was in Hera's shop, and she was there so—"

"You met Hera, too?" he said in an awed tone.

"Perfect! Your friendship with that power couple could be an asset to us."

"Us?" And what did he mean by an asset? She wasn't exactly friends with them. She'd only met the . . . um . . . *power couple* once.

Narcissus beamed at her, showing his beautiful white teeth. "Sure. You and me—we're a team. You're the only nymph I'd ever trust to be my fashion designer."

Pleased, Echo smiled back. She hadn't known he valued her so much!

Tiresias sidled up to Narcissus just then. "Don't forget me. Your team needs a stylist," he said, sounding like he was feeling a little left out.

When Narcissus only nodded at him distractedly, Echo gave the stylist an encouraging smile. "Right, we're a three-person team."

"I only wish we'd been able to bring our artist along," Narcissus mused. "We're missing some great ops for modeling shots, posing with some of these immortals we've been meeting."

"There'll be other opportunities," Echo said mildly as she set her tray in the return. When it came to his desired career, Narcissus had a one-track mind. But focus and determination were good character traits, right?

"Yeah, like at the IM tomorrow," said Narcissus, perking up. "It's our big chance."

"Big chance for what?" Lifting an eyebrow in confusion, Echo looked between the two boys.

"He's talking about the parade," Tiresias informed her as the three of them headed out of the cafeteria.

"It's the chance of a lifetime," Narcissus enthused. "Because guess what? I will be starring on the main float—the final and grandest one of the entire parade!"

"Really?" breathed Echo. "How did—"

"Really!" Narcissus confirmed before she could finish asking how the invitation had come about. "And I want *you* to be at my side," he said, dramatically swinging an arm wide.

"Huh? Really?" Echo said again, hardly able to believe it.

"Yup! This parade is shaping up to be the social event of the season!" Narcissus positively glowed with pleasure. "And that final float is the one that'll get the most attention," he went on. "I'm told that Zeus and his two nannies will be on it."

"Evergreen!" said Echo. His enthusiasm was catching, she thought as he and Tiresias led her toward the front doors of the Academy.

"Before the parade tomorrow I'll scout out reporters covering the event at the IM and make sure they know you're going to be Zeus's special parade guests," Tiresias said now. "I want you guys to be drawn by dozens of artists and pictured in every publication. *Teen Scrollazine, Greekly Weekly News*—you name it." For emphasis he used the thumbs and forefingers of both his hands to form a box-shaped frame, through which he viewed them as he hoped the artists would the following day.

Echo cocked her head at Narcissus. "But I don't get it. Why were we invited onto Zeus's float?"

"You're a nymph! Like those nannies of his, Melissa and Amalthea. You'll fit right in," he told her, as if that explained all. Then he went on dreamily, "Just think! That fashion designer Moda is bound to see drawings of me in the news after this, and he'll want to hire me as a model." Glancing at her, he added magnanimously, "Oh, and of course I'll tell Moda about you, so you can get into the fashion world too."

"Wow, you'd do that for me?" Narcissus must really like her, since he was ambitious for her as well as for himself. She nodded toward his stylist. "And you'll talk to Moda about Tiresias, too?"

"Natch!" Narcissus said, pausing inside MOA's bronze front doors. "Only thing is, none of this will work unless we have the right clothes." He looked at her appraisingly. "We need showstoppers to wear in that parade. Lots of bling."

"I could sew outfits!" Echo exclaimed. "I'll just rush home and . . ." Her voice trailed off. What kind of welcome would she get back in the forest? She kind of wondered if some of her old friends might secretly be glad to be rid of her. Because maybe they didn't want to think about the problem of what to do with her now that she didn't have a tree. Was she ready to find out? Maybe not, she decided.

She did miss FirHeart, though, and Daphne and Pan. A little ache formed in her heart. Eager to chase it away, she pounced on Narcissus's parade costume idea. "I'll scout around for materials to sew something here at MOA. Artemis and her friends might—" she began.

"No time for that," Narcissus interrupted. He walked over to the basket of winged sandals, grabbed a pair, and handed them to her. "You'll need to borrow some outfits from Hera's shop instead."

"Me? Borrow?" Echo repeated. How would showcasing outfits from that shop help her get noticed as a fashion designer? But he was right that there wasn't enough time to gather materials and decide on a

164

design for his and hers outfits. So there wasn't really any other option. "Okay. I'll ask her. Since we're in the parade, I bet she'll be up for it."

"No, don't *ask*!" Narcissus said quickly.

"We want this to be a total surprise for Hera," Tiresias put in. "Showcasing her outfits on the main float will be great promo for her shop. She'll love it!"

Echo sent him an uncertain look as the two boys ushered her outside. "But won't her shop already have a float of its own in the parade?"

"Rumor has it that she and her staff have been too busy with the upcoming wedding to prepare a float. You don't want her shop to be left out, do you?" Narcissus asked her earnestly. "You'll be doing her a favor!"

"Well, when you put it that way . . . ," said Echo.

Narcissus grinned at her. "All you have to do is

pick out the most awesome outfits you can find in Hera's shop, and we'll return them after the celebration. Easy-peasy."

"Oh, and make sure Narcissus's complements his eyes and skin tone," Tiresias put in.

"Okay," Echo agreed. "But we'd better get going if we want to reach the IM before they close." Putting a hand against a wall for balance, she slipped on one winged sandal, then the other. Her flying skills probably weren't powerful enough to wing two mortals to the IM as well as herself. She was about to tell them this, when Narcissus spoke.

"We'll stay put. We trust you to get the job done," he told her. "Besides, we already have plans here tonight. Some Beauty-ology students will be giving me a facial and a hair trim so that I'll look my best for the big day. In turn they'll get extra credit for their work."

"Remember not to look at yourself in any mirrors while the students are working, though," Tiresias reminded him as the two boys turned to go.

"Yeah, yeah," Narcissus assured him, rolling his eyes. Then he called back to Echo, "We're staying in the boys' dorm in a spare room tonight. Just come up to the fifth floor and knock on the hall door when you're back with the you-know-what, and someone will come get me. Remember, this is supposed to be a surprise. Tell no one."

Once the front doors had shut the two boys inside the Academy, Echo flew off to the Immortal Marketplace on her own. The sun would be setting in a couple of hours. She'd have just long enough to borrow a couple of outfits, then fly back to MOA before darkness fell.

Unfortunately, she hadn't realized that the IM was

closing early because of the parade the next day. By the time she arrived at Hera's Happy Endings, Hera was gone, and her assistants were getting ready to leave too. She considered enlightening them about the plan to borrow two outfits to promote the shop in the parade, but Narcissus had told her not to tell anyone.

That was probably wise. The assistants might let the plan slip to Hera, and that would ruin the surprise. Besides, from the way they frowned at Echo when she entered the shop, she figured they were feeling tired and grumpy. After all, they'd been working long hours to get ready for Monday's wedding. What if they refused her request? She couldn't risk it. However, she didn't know how she was going to sneak anything out of the shop without them noticing.

At the last minute some customers arrived. As the assistants got busy with them, Echo paced among the

168

racks of formal chitons and tunics, her thoughts racing.

Finally, she paused before a beautiful long, white wedding chiton with flounces of delicate netting that the sales tag called tulle. The gown was stunningly beautiful. She tried to imagine the young bride who might choose it. What would she be like? Echo couldn't bring a picture of anyone in particular to mind, however. Though the gown was gorgeous, it just didn't seem one-of-a-kind—meant for one *special* bride. For that the chiton would need pizzazz. Bling, as Narcissus had called it.

Then, on a low table beside the rack, she spotted books with ideas for jazzing up the shop's sample chitons. Oh, that explained it. These chitons were all meant to be given finishing touches that would make each one truly a bride's own. Suddenly an idea struck her. What if she copied an idea from the books to add special touches to this particular chiton? And to a matching tunic for Narcissus as well. That way she could showcase Hera's store samples while also proving her own talent as a designer?

Excitement filled her at the thought of the task she'd set herself. She loved fashion, and the idea of making the sample dress exactly as beautiful as one in the book thrilled her. But then she heard a *click*, and her shoulders drooped. There was no time for what she had in mind. The assistants had begun locking up for the night.

What should she do? Narcissus had entrusted this job to her. It was really important to him. She'd already let FirHeart down. She didn't want to let Narcissus down too. He was counting on her.

Panicking, she crouched low so the assistants wouldn't catch sight of her. Then she silently made her way to the storage closet where she and Zeus had talked that morning. She slipped through the curtain to hide.

Once Hera's employees were gone, Echo crept back out into the main shop again. The candles in the overhead chandeliers had *poofed* out the moment the assistants had gone. Fortunately, rows of safety torches along the walls now magically lit themselves to serve as night-lights. She grabbed the sample chiton and a matching tunic. Both were a little big for her and Narcissus, so she would have to temporarily take in their seams.

In the back of the shop, she found scissors, pins, needles, thread, ribbon, measuring tapes, and pattern-making paper. And tons of sparkly bling, such as sequins and rhinestones. It was designer heaven! Fueled by her passion for fashion, she got to work.

After a few hours her stomach rumbled. "Even fashion designers need more than just the thrill of creating a new outfit to fuel them," she murmured to herself. She needed a snack pronto! She'd spied more cupcakes in the storage area when she'd hidden there earlier. However, they and all the other snacks that had been in the shop were now inside a locked glass cabinet. Echo dug through some drawers under the cabinet, hoping to find a key, but came up empty.

Just as she was about to give up on the snack idea, she spotted a platter with a dome-shaped glass lid. It was sitting on a shelf high above the locked cabinet, and held a lone yellow cupcake. Thank godness it had been overlooked when Hera had locked the others away.

She could kind of understand why Zeus had found these cupcakes irresistible, she thought as she reached up to nab it. This one looked especially yummy, with thick, creamy lemon frosting on top. She munched away, then got back to her stitching.

At the crack of dawn one of Hera's employees opened the shop. A tired Echo sneaked out the door when the assistant's back was turned. She headed back to MOA with one clothing bag under each arm. After she ducked in through the bronze front doors, she tiptoed up to the fourth-floor girls' dorm. Following Artemis's directions from the day before, she crept down the girls' hall, then silently slipped into Artemis's room.

The minute she shut the door behind her, a blood-hound, a beagle, and a greyhound came bounding over to her. All three dogs jumped around happily, their tongues hanging out.

"Shh!" Echo told them. She glanced over at the

sleeping girl on one side of the room. Artemis was apparently used to such disturbances, and merely rolled over without waking up.

Echo found her way to one of the closets. It was stuffed full of clothes, all hung neatly, with no room for more. She tried the other closet. There were far fewer chitons here, but most were half on and half off their hangers, and some were even balled up on the floor of the closet. It was as if Artemis had a split personality when it came to how she cared for her clothes. Still, there was plenty of room in this closet, so she hung her and Narcissus's outfits at its far end. Then she sank down onto the empty bed opposite Artemis's and conked out.

9

The Parade

*W*HAP! ECHO WOKE WITH A START AS A DOOR
slammed shut. She had fallen asleep quickly after
sneaking into Artemis's dorm room earlier that
morning, but was still groggy after working all night
in Hera's store.

"Oops, sorry. I didn't meet to close it so hard,"
Artemis said. She'd just breezed into the dorm room
with her dogs, and was carrying a tray.

Echo blinked at the bright light streaming in through the window on the far wall, which looked out onto the courtyard. Outside, the sun was already high in the sky!

"Figured you must have been out late, since you weren't here when I went to bed," Artemis said cheerfully. "In case you're wondering, it's midmorning." As usual, her dogs were bouncing around the room with excitement.

"Midmorning?" Echo sat up and gathered the covers around her. That meant she'd only been asleep about four hours. Stretching her arms high, she yawned. Then she reached over to pet the dogs, gently pushing them away when they tried to jump onto her bed. The greyhound grabbed one end of a chew toy, and a game of tug-of-war began between him and the beagle.

"Mm-hm. I've already taken my dogs out and had breakfast."

"Breakfast?" Echo repeated.

"Afraid you're too late for that, sleepyhead," Artemis informed her. "But don't worry, I brought you some Ambrosia-O's cereal and milk from the cafeteria." As she brought the tray over to Echo, she asked, "So anyway, where were you last night?"

Echo yawned again, sitting up straighter to take the tray onto her lap. "Last night?" As she opened the carton of milk and poured some over her bowl of cereal, she tried to think up an excuse for where she'd been. She didn't really want to lie, but she'd promised Narcissus not to spill the beans. Luckily, a knock at the door saved her from having to come up with something to say. It was a special knock—two knuckle raps, a wait, then three quick raps.

"Aphrodite's secret knock," Artemis informed Echo as she dug into her cereal. Then in a louder voice Artemis called out, "Come in!"

Aphrodite entered Artemis's room wearing a flouncy pink-and-white chiton with sparkles along its hem. She dashed to the stuffed-full, neat closet Echo had tried first earlier that morning. "Hi, guys. Sorry to barge in. I need something for today's parade. And I think it's here somewhere." She began pushing things around on the closet's high shelf.

"I only need one closet, so I let Aphrodite use my second one since the two closets in her room aren't enough for all her clothes," Artemis explained as she roughhoused with her dogs on the rug between the beds.

Aha, thought Echo. So that was why the closets

178

looked so different. She guessed no one would accuse Artemis of being a neatnik.

After a few seconds Aphrodite emerged from her tidy, stuffed closet holding a half-circle silver band studded with sparkly pink stones. "Here it is! My tiara."

"Tiara?" echoed Echo. Pushing the coverlet off, she sat cross-legged and kept eating.

"Too much?" Aphrodite asked the two girls uncertainly. She set it on her head and turned this way and that, surveying herself in the full-length mirror that hung on the closet door. Seeing her, Echo was suddenly glad of her choice of dress for today's event, because it would fit right in with the fanciness of Aphrodite's.

"I like it. It matches the sparkles in your chiton," said Artemis. Then she added, "On the other hand, what I know about fashion could fit into Echo's spoon."

Aphrodite laughed. "True," she said affectionately. "But in this case I agree. It *is* a good match. I'll wear it!"

Echo nodded her approval as she set her empty bowl aside. Aphrodite sent her a smile. Then her gaze slid over the golden-edged red chiton Artemis was wearing, eyeing it critically. Seeming to deem it suitable for the day, her bright blue gaze switched to the rumpled chiton Echo was wearing. She'd been so tired last night, she'd slept in it.

"Feel free to borrow anything you want from my closet for the IM parade today," Aphrodite offered.

Echo yawned again, nodding. "IM parade today?"

"Yeah," Artemis told her. "Athena's already at the marketplace with Persephone. We need to get going." She raised an eyebrow. "Aphrodite and I will wait for you if you can get ready fast."

"Fast?" Echo shook her head to show that wasn't

possible. Suddenly she frowned. It had just occurred to her that ever since she'd awakened this morning, she'd been repeating the ends of everyone else's sentences. Weird!

"Okay, if you're sure." Pausing at the door, Aphrodite pointed down the hall. "So, the bathroom's that way. Everything you'll need is already in there. And, like I said, my closet is your closet for as long as you're here at MOA. Feel free to borrow."

Before Echo could thank her, the three dogs bounded down the hall ahead of the two goddessgirls. "We're off, then. See you there!" said Artemis. Waving bye, the two girls dashed away.

"See you there!" Echo called after them. There she went again—repeating the ends of sentences. Maybe it was just because she hadn't quite woken up yet. She hopped up and scurried down the hall toward the bathroom. The hall was superquiet. Every girl in the dorm must've already left for the Immortal Marketplace. She'd better get a move on!

But when she was halfway to the bathroom, the door at the end of the hall opened partway. A boy's head peeked in. "*Psst!* It's me, Narcissus."

Echo let out a squeak of surprise, but then she calmed down. "Narcissus?"

He nodded, then craned his neck to look around the hall with interest. His dark-lashed eyes flicked to the NO BOYS ALLOWED sign posted on the wall just inside the door. Heeding the sign, he stayed put. "So?" he called to her in a whisper.

Echo shrugged uncertainly, not sure what he was asking. "So?"

"Where are they? Did you get them last night? Our outfits?"

"Our outfits?" said Echo. She tried to make her mouth form other words. Words to explain about how she'd spent the night adding pizzazz to the outfits each of them would wear today, and how she had gotten in too late to wake him. But she couldn't make any such explanation come out.

Narcissus frowned. "Are you mocking me?"

"Mocking? Me?" said Echo, raising her brows. She shook her head earnestly, trying to get across the message that, no, she was not mocking him. Not *intentionally*, anyway. Something was definitely wrong. Why could she only repeat the last words of what others said?

Narcissus rolled his eyes. "Whatever. Have you got my tunic?"

She made another attempt to tell him everything, but when she felt his words, "my tunic," bubbling into

183

her mouth, she swallowed them before they were uttered. Instead she held a finger to her lips, as if to say he needed to be quiet in case others were still in their rooms and overheard. Then she gestured for him to stay where he was and pointed down the hall, indicating that she'd go get his outfit and return in a minute.

Hoping her speech would be back to normal soon, she zipped down the hall to Artemis's room and whipped open the messy closet where she'd hung the two outfits from Hera's shop. She grabbed the tunic and chiton she'd hung at the far end. Each was still wrapped in a papyrus bag.

Next she found a notescroll and a pre-inked feather pen on Artemis's desk. She tried to write a note to Narcissus saying that she had lost her voice and would meet him at the IM. That way she wouldn't run the risk of seeming to mock him again. However, her message didn't come out as intended. Instead she watched her hand write, *Got my tunic?* Those were the very last words Narcissus had spoken to her a minute ago!

Had she caught some weird kind of copycat virus that was going around? Or maybe, instead of a virus, it was some strange allergic reaction to Artemis's dogs? Guiltily she wondered next if it could be a magic punishment for "borrowing" outfits from Hera without asking.

After tossing the useless message into the trash, Echo dashed up the hall and wordlessly handed the tunic bag to Narcissus. She smiled, hoping he wouldn't ask her any more questions. She didn't want to embarrass herself by repeating things again. Luckily for her, he was totally fixated on getting a glimpse of his new outfit.

"Awesome!" he enthused, peeking inside the bag. "Can't wait to try it on. I'll meet you at the IM."

"Meet you at the IM," she agreed, nodding. *Argh!* What was wrong with her? Maybe she should just stay here until this copycat virus-allergy-curse thing wore off. But no, she wanted to show off her new gown and help Hera's shop. Besides, Narcissus needed her at his side to complement his outfit.

Once he was gone, Echo dashed into the bathroom and hung her fancy new chiton on a hook on the wall. Then she turned and caught sight of herself in the mirror. *Eek!* Not only was the chiton she'd slept in a wrinkled mess, but her green hair looked like a long, tangled bird's nest. And the perfect, handsome Narcissus had just seen her like this. *Double eek!*

She hopped into the shower. It took her a few seconds to figure out how to turn it on, since she wasn't used to bathrooms with smooth silver mirrors and showers with gold handles and spigots. Back in the forest she and her friends showered under trickling waterfalls, and you had to look at the surface of a pond to view your reflection.

Once she was dressed, she surveyed her wet hair with displeasure. It was going to take forever to dry. But when she found a brush in a supply cabinet and began using it, a brisk breeze whipped up. It was a magic brush that blew her hair dry in seconds!

Within a half hour she was ready to go. Gazing at herself in the mirror, her jaw dropped. Wow! The chiton had transformed her. It made her look as amazing as a . . . a . . . goddessgirl! She had copied the picture in that book from Hera's shop down to every last detail, adding sequins and sparkly gems to the satin part of the gown, mostly around the neckline and hem. She remembered Aphrodite's earlier question about the tiara—"Too much?" Echo couldn't help wondering if she should ask the same question about this chiton.

Well, so what if it was over-the-top? She'd probably never again get a chance to wear something so fancy! Before hurrying downstairs, she grabbed the simple cloak she'd also stuffed into the clothing bag she'd brought from Hera's shop. It would help keep her dress a secret before the unveiling on the float.

Soon she was zooming through the air wearing winged sandals, on her way to the Immortal Marketplace, her frilly skirt fanning out behind her. As she approached the IM, the skies around her filled with chariots bringing immortal guests from other realms. And below her, crowds of mortals were making their way to the IM too. There was a big grandstand with dignitaries and musicians at the marketplace entrance, where the parade would end with the final float's arrival. It looked like Zeus's event was going to be a big thumbs-up!

After touching down, Echo tethered the wings on her sandals and wandered among the floats. They were all in a line that stretched around the IM, ready to begin parading. She hurried down the line, looking them over.

There was one from a store called Gods' Gift that was shaped like a giant gift box tied with an enormous satin bow. Artfully arranged atop it were decorations that included papyrus-tissue wedding bells and regular-size gift boxes with elaborate wrappings. Now and then puppet heads popped up from the smaller boxes to harmonize in the singing of a song about the joy of gift giving. Echo found herself repeating their silly song, and unable to stop. How embarrassing! She rushed on.

The Oracle-O Bakery and Scrollbooks float was shaped like a giant papyrus scroll, Echo saw as she came even with it. Cassandra already stood atop it, readying baskets of tasty giveaway cookies. Each cookie was in a little net bag tied with a ribbon. Those free samples would be sought-after prizes that were were sure to benefit the shop, bringing customers in for additional cookies, and scrollbooks, too.

Just then the parade got underway. As the floats rolled out, Cassandra began to toss the net cookie bags into the waiting audience. Hands reached, hoping to catch one.

The man in the yellow-and-black checkered suit that Echo had overheard in Hera's shop was driving the next float in line, from a store called Be a Hero.

It had shields fastened in a row on all sides, bearing the likenesses of various heroes, such as Heracles and Odysseus.

Yet another float from a store called Mighty Fighty was shaped like a single giant, athletic winged sandal. Pairs of sandals were even magically circling in the air above the float, swooping and soaring like birds! Echo scampered on, searching for the final float.

A few breathless minutes later she found it. Tiresias was already standing near the float, which hadn't yet begun to move forward. He was busily writing (more glowing descriptions of Narcissus, perhaps?) in the blue fan scrollbook.

Echo gazed up at the grand float and gasped. It was *sooo* beautiful, shaped like a giant white layered wedding cake with little flowers, birds, and other designs sculpted out of fake icing all around its edges. Unfortunately, an enthusiastic crowd had gathered so close that she couldn't see well enough to tell if Narcissus was already atop it. But surely he had to be up there by now.

Abruptly the float lurched forward, and she lost sight of Tiresias in the crowd. At the same time a volley of flat thunderbolt-shaped medallions made of real gold, with *MOA* stamped on them, flew out from over the sides of the float. "Here you go!" Zeus's voice boomed as bystanders leaped to catch the bolts.

She was about to call up and ask Zeus how she was supposed to get onto the float, when a small door down low opened along the float's side. A hand reached out, waving her over. "Hurry! Get in!"

Lifting the skirt of her gown, she leaped inside. An excited Narcissus was waiting for her in a compartment at the base of the float, which contained stairs leading upward. He shut the door behind her, then said, "Did you hear the news? Moda's here!"

"Here?" Echo echoed, looking around the small area.

"In the crowd, I mean! Isn't it cool? His is the final word in fashion," said Narcissus. "And he's going to *L-O-V-E love* this tunic you got me. It's perfection! Once I impress him, my career is made!" He did a little happy dance. A *very* little dance, since there wasn't much room in the cramped space.

Echo dared to hope that Moda would be impressed not just by Narcissus's modeling, but by her work, and Hera's samples, too!

"Shh! Keep quiet," Narcissus whispered as their float lurched into even faster motion.

Fine by me, she thought. She *wanted* to keep quiet. At least until her copycat speech allergy went away!

"When I say go, we run up the stairs and pop out of the top of this cake," Narcissus went on.

How fun! And dramatic. She loved the idea. It had probably been Zeus's, since, according to articles she'd read about him, he was skilled at generating mega-amazing ideas. Echo whipped off her cape, getting ready for the big moment. Once they popped out, they'd be a matched set, like a bride and groom decoration on top of a wedding cake!

Their float rumbled along, pulled by four strong, glossy horses. Inside the float Echo was getting more and more excited. If their outfits were a success, maybe she really would find a new home in the fashion world! Then, instead of going to live with some other group of nymphs, she could hang out with Narcissus.

"Almost time. Okay . . . ," Narcissus whispered. "Now!" On his cue, they ran up the stairs.

But when the two of them lifted the lid on the top tier of the fake cake and popped out, they came face-to-face with Hera and a group of others standing around it. Narcissus grabbed Echo's hand and raised their arms high. "Surprise!" he yelled. Then he struck a modeling pose. Below in the crowd, the artists and reporters from *Greekly Weekly* and *Teen Scrollazine* rapidly sketched them both.

Instantly Echo sensed that something was not right. She turned in a circle, studying those around her. There was Hera, Melissa, Amalthea, and Ide, with a young man who must be Ide's fiancé. And of course Zeus! They did not look happy. But they *did* look surprised. All at once the reason for their mood hit her. Just as he'd lied about rescuing Artemis in the Forest of the Beasts, Narcissus had also lied about getting permission for the two of them to be on this float!

"What kind of stunt is this? Explain!" Zeus roared, confirming her suspicion. So that was why Narcissus had asked her not to tell anyone of his plan. Because he had crashed the parade! And she'd unwittingly helped him.

And then things got worse. Hera gasped suddenly, staring at Echo's chiton. "Oh no!"

"Oh no!" Ide repeated, her eyes going wide. Had Melissa's daughter caught the copycat virus too? Echo wondered. But then Ide pointed an accusing finger at her and spoke words that weren't repeats. "That's my gown!" she exclaimed.

"My gown?" Echo echoed. She glanced in confusion at the chiton Ide was wearing. It was completely different from hers. So what was this bride-to-be talking about?

Ide's fiancé obviously didn't understand either. He

was staring at Echo with a puzzled look on his face. Before anyone could step in to explain, Ide burst into tears. "She's wearing my bridal chiton!"

"My bridal chiton?" Echo repeated.

"It's not yours! It is . . . *was* mine," wailed Ide. "Now I can't wear it on Monday after all. Everyone knows that nobody is supposed to see a bride's gown before the wedding."

"She's right," confirmed Melissa, frowning at Echo. "Especially not the groom! It's bad luck."

"My wedding is ruined!" Hysterical now, the honey-haired Ide collapsed into her mother's arms, sobbing.

"But I thought you'd already picked up your gown from Hera's shop? How could this cake-popping nymph have gotten hold of it?" Amalthea asked Ide.

Melissa, who was patting her daughter's back,

explained. "Ide dropped it off again at Hera's shop for a few final alterations yesterday."

Ide whirled around and pointed an angry finger at Hera. "I can't believe you let *someone else* wear *my* gown on this float. What a cheap publicity stunt! I'm going to tell all my friends never to shop at the Immortal Marketplace, and especially not at Hera's Happy Endings!" Looking devastated, she scrambled down from the float and ran off. Her groom quickly followed her, as did Melissa and Amalthea. Which left Echo and Narcissus to deal with Hera and Zeus.

10

Copycake

ZEUS'S BLUE EYES NARROWED TO SLITS AS HE stared at Echo. "You stole Ide's wedding chiton from Hera's shop?"

Wishing she could melt into a puddle, Echo desperately shook her head.

"No?" Hera asked, raising her eyebrows.

"No!" Echo repeated. If only she could explain herself. Not being able to talk properly was a nightmare!

Why didn't Narcissus speak up? He was the one who'd gotten them into this mess, after all.

From the frown on Hera's face it was clear she didn't believe Echo. And Zeus looked ready to bean her with one of his infamous thunderbolts. They thought this was Ide's actual wedding chiton she was wearing. It wasn't, though. She'd found this one still unadorned, hanging on the rack with a price tag. But apparently the pattern for the finishing touches Echo had chosen from the book had been the same pattern Ide had chosen. Talk about bad luck!

How could she communicate this information? She tried to mime the act of sewing decorations on the sample dress she was wearing, but everyone only looked at her like she was as nutty as the walnut trees in her forest back home.

And there was no way Echo could inform them

that she had only borrowed outfits to help Hera and Narcissus. And maybe herself too, if she were being honest. She felt upset that she and Narcissus had managed to ruin Ide's wedding day, even though it had been an accident.

She glanced over at the silent boy, her eyes pleading with him to speak up, since she was unable to. Finally he opened his mouth. "It's her fault," he said, pointing at Echo and backing away.

"Her fault?" said Echo, blinking at him.

"This was all Echo's idea," Narcissus went on, carefully avoiding her eyes. "I asked her to find outfits for us, but that was only to promote Hera's Happy Endings. I didn't know she'd steal the bride's wedding chiton!"

As Narcissus spoke, Zeus's eyebrows rammed together and he glared harder at Echo. She squeezed her eyes shut, expecting to be incinerated by a thunderbolt at any second.

"Our deal's off!" he roared at her. "I'm not going to help you with switching realms now. Not after you hurt Ide and embarrassed Hera and me in front of all of Mount Olympus, and possibly even ruined relations with visiting dignitaries. This celebration was supposed to bring shoppers to the IM. But your shenanigans have not helped matters."

Echo gulped and nodded. She completely understood. Not just what Zeus was saying but also that Narcissus was a *rat*. To save his own skin he'd shifted the blame to her. And he actually appeared to believe that she had knowingly stolen a dress belonging to someone else. That really hurt!

Just then their float gave a hard lurch. They'd arrived at the entrance to the Immortal Marketplace, where colorful flags flew and dignitaries from other realms awaited Zeus's speech to signal the end of the parade. Everyone was staring. Because of Narcissus and Echo's "surprise," their float had become the center of attention in a bigger way than anyone could have anticipated.

Zeus forced a huge smile and turned to address the enormous crowd that had gathered around the cake float. "I hope you all enjoyed the parade!" he called out in his hearty booming voice. "I encourage you, one and all, to enter the Immortal Marketplace and explore the vast array of shops within. You'll find free gifts and exciting new products every-where. Don't forget to visit the grand opening of Good Nannies Honey & Milk, a new shop owned and operated by my nannies, Melissa and Amalthea. Tell your friends to come too!"

As he did his best to proclaim the virtues of shopping at the IM, Hera waved Echo and Narcissus off the float. Before they left, though, Echo spotted news reporters fleeing right in the middle of Zeus's speech. No doubt they were eager to get to work writing articles about the bridal disaster she'd helped cause.

Like the rat he was, Narcissus ran down the stairs ahead of her, leaving the sinking ship, er, float. Then he disappeared into the crowd, taking Tiresias with him.

Noticing Hera heading for her shop, Echo started to follow. Somehow she had to fix things!

But before she could catch up to Hera, a familiar voice called out, "Hey!" Echo halted in her tracks. It was Pan! He zoomed over to her, wearing winged sandals like those she'd seen on the Mighty Fighty float. He must've bought some at that shop.

"Hey!" she repeated, impressed at how easily he

banked around the crowds of people milling about. He'd gotten good at flying fast!

"Daphne said to tell you she's sorry she couldn't come with me," Pan said when he stopped beside her. "She didn't think she could make it all the way to MOA and back to the fo-fo-forest again in twenty-four hours before her chant to protect LaurelRing wore off."

Echo nodded, understanding. She'd almost forgotten she'd sent him a wingscroll message suggesting he come here today so that she could help him meet Apollo.

"So," said Pan, looking around. "Is Apollo ah-ah-around here anywhere?" he bleated. "I brought a new flute I ma-a-ade that I want to show him."

Echo didn't really have time for this right now, but there was no way for her to explain that, of course.

205

Quickly she looked around for Apollo. Seeing him near the bandstand at the IM entrance, she pulled Pan over to meet him. Unable to speak properly, she reached for the flute Pan was carrying and began miming the playing of it, making a total fool out of herself in the process.

"I think she wants you to audition for me," Apollo told Pan, chuckling. She guessed that he'd been performing music with his band here at the entrance during the entire parade and hadn't yet heard about the trouble she'd caused. Well, she certainly wasn't going to tell him . . . not that she *could* have.

Overlooking her weird antics, Pan put his modified flute to his mouth and began playing, his fingers flying. He played well, but the sounds that issued forth from the flute were thin and had an unfortunate nasal quality to them.

"Sorry, shepherd-dude. That just won't cut it," Apollo informed him kindly but honestly.

Pan's shoulders sagged. But even Echo had been able to tell that his instrument's sound wasn't a good one.

"It's not you," Apollo assured him. "Your talent is mega-phenomenal. You just need to find a better instrument with a brilliant sound that'll showcase that talent."

Pan nodded, looking disheartened. "I've been thinking the sa-a-ame thing."

As the two boys continued talking music and some of Apollo's band friends joined them, Echo eased away. Because now she had to go face the music in Hera's shop. And she suspected that that music wasn't going to sound half as good as Pan's had!

When she finally made it into the IM, the first

thing she heard as she pushed through the door to Hera's Happy Endings was an unhappy shop assistant. "It's terrible what happened," he was saying to Hera. "Everyone at the IM worked so hard to contribute to the festivities and get the word out to mortals that they are welcome here."

Argh! Not only had Echo ruined Ide's upcoming big day, it sounded like she'd also ruined the whole IM promotion. Because of her, all the attention had gotten focused on the trouble on the final float. If stores really did fail, she'd feel awful! Since no one had noticed her yet, she crept closer to listen in.

"There's nothing to be done about that for now, so let's discuss the problem of Ide's wedding chiton," Hera began in a confident, reassuring tone. "Now, what can we do to put things right?"

"I don't know. Her wedding is only two days away,"

worried a second shop assistant. She shook her head doubtfully.

"We can only do our best and hope she'll give us a second chance," Hera said. "The first time around Ide chose the dress she wanted. It looked wonderful on Echo, but as we all know, it wasn't really the best style for Ide."

Huh? This was news to Echo.

"So this time let's do the choosing instead," Hera went on. "We'll come up with something we think is right for Ide and present it to her."

"But remember how difficult it was to get her to make a decision on that first chiton? There was no talking her into something more appropriate," put in an assistant.

"More appropriate," Echo murmured unhappily.

Everyone in the shop turned to look at her in

surprise. Seeing the gown she was wearing, the assistants instantly guessed who she was. They scowled at her.

Hera frowned too, looking annoyed at her intrusion into their conversation. "What are you doing here?" she asked.

"Doing here," Echo repeated, since it was the only thing she could say.

Slowly, understanding dawned in Hera's eyes. "Wait a minute," she told Echo. "Say something else."

Echo sighed. "Something else."

"Is that supposed to be a joke?" one of the assistants said hotly.

"A joke," Echo repeated unhappily.

"Humph!" said another assistant. "Well, it's not a very funny one!"

"Never mind that," Hera said quickly. "Tell me,

Echo. Did you eat something in this shop before you took Ide's gown? Maybe a lemon-frosted yellow cupcake?"

"Cupcake." Echo nodded. Only, what did eating that cupcake have to do with anything?

Hera snapped her fingers. "That explains your repeat-speak, then. That cupcake was an enchanted copycake. A trap meant for Zeus. To teach him a lesson in case he ignored my warning about not eating sweets for a week and came back for more cupcakes."

"More cupcakes!" Echo blurted, even though she wasn't hungry.

Hera sighed. "The copycake's effects should wear off within a few hours. Till then I'm afraid you'll be able only to repeat others' words."

Feeling frustrated, Echo looked around wildly, hoping to spot Ide's actual gown. She wanted to prove to Hera that she hadn't really taken it. But it was probably in some special closet for gowns needing alterations. Echo had no clue where that might be. If only they'd go check instead of assuming she was a thief.

As Hera went back to discussing a new gown for Ide with her assistants, Echo turned to go, feeling totally frustrated and down in the dumps. Secretly she resolved to help Hera if she could, however. She owed her that. But right now it seemed an overwhelming task.

Outside the IM she found Pan listening to Heavens Above perform up on the bandstand. "I think I'll head back to the forest," he said when he saw her. Certain that she'd worn out her welcome at MOA and having no place else to go, Echo went with him. Absorbed in their own thoughts, they didn't talk much as they winged homeward. That was just as well, since she was still suffering from the effects of the copycake she'd unwittingly eaten.

By early afternoon Echo was growing nervous about the kind of reception she would get now that they were nearing home. As they crossed through the Forest of the Beasts, lightning suddenly shot out from the labyrinth, whizzing past them to scorch some ferns.

"Wha-a-at the . . . ," Pan bleated, looking at her in surprise.

That lightning had come at them sideways, Echo realized with a start, just like the bolt that had hit FirHeart. Immediately she flew into the maze, leaving Pan to follow. She was going to get to the bottom of this!

Two dozen turns later she and Pan found themselves

at the entrance to the labyrinth's central courtyard. Hearing voices, they hid behind some bushes to listen in.

Narcissus and Tiresias were inside the labyrinth, standing next to the Pool of Magic along with Anaxandra, their artist. There was another girl with them too—Syrinx!

Tiresias was tinkering with the Drakon, which stood silent and upright. "Phew! Looks like this beast is finally fixed," he was saying. "Almost got us with that last shower of sparks, but I think I've got it under control again."

"Good work," said Anaxandra. "Okay, so let's go back to our original plan and get a sketch of Narcissus pretending to fight it. Then we'll send my sketchscrolls to Moda."

"Yeah! Those plus the drawings the reporters'

artists made of me jumping out of Zeus's cake float ought to really wow him," Narcissus said approvingly.

Tiresias nodded. "Those float pics will probably hit the front pages of *GW* and the *'Zine* tomorrow."

"Cool," said Syrinx. The river nymph smiled adoringly at Narcissus, but he didn't even notice. Typical.

Syrinx was crushing! Echo realized in surprise. She glanced to the side at Pan, who had noticed too. Poor guy. His crush on Syrinx had just been crushed.

"So turn that Drakon on again!" said Narcissus, striking his spear-the-beast pose.

"But wouldn't that be dangerous?" Syrinx said. "You might get injured."

"She's right," said Tiresias. "You're a model, and your looks are your fortune! Ours too, for that matter. Remember what happened a few days ago?"

Narcissus shrugged. "Last time we didn't know

how it worked. I think we've got the hang of it now, don't you?"

"But we still can't control the size or direction of its sparks," noted Anaxandra, gazing doubtfully at the Drakon.

"Sparks, schmarks." Narcissus laughed and glanced over at Syrinx. "They're more like lightning bolts, really," he told her. "The other day one of them hit a tree before we could turn this beast off. Cut it right in two. We could hear it fall even at a distance. *Ka-Boom!*" He laughed again. "Good thing it was just a tree. No real harm done."

Echo and Pan stared at each other, appalled. To her credit, Syrinx hadn't found Narcissus's comment amusing either. She was staring at him as if she couldn't believe he'd said that.

Echo's cheeks flamed in anger. "Just a tree? No

real harm done?" she repeated, jumping out of the bushes to confront Narcissus. But after saying those words, she said no more. It was impossible to continue scolding him till the copycake's effects wore off!

"What are you doing here?" Syrinx demanded. Her eyes took in Echo's outfit. "And what's with the fancy chiton? Where'd you copy this one from?"

As usual, her words caused pinpricks of unhappiness to stab Echo's heart. But then she saw that Syrinx was wearing a very familiar chiton. One Echo had made herself and managed to recover after the FirHeart disaster. This sneak must've found it in the makeshift hut and "borrowed" it.

Noticing where Echo was looking, Syrinx quickly defended her borrowing. "Haven't you heard? I'll be staying on in the forest. I've decided to become a

Dryad. Since I'm basically your replacement, I borrowed your stuff. No one thought you'd dare come back here after what you did to your tree."

Echo took a step backward, feeling as if she'd just been slapped. At the same time Daphne burst into the labyrinth's center, joining them.

"That's totally not true, Syrinx. You don't have any intention of becoming a Dryad, and you know it." Without waiting for a response, Daphne gave Echo a hug, telling her, "I was waiting for Pan to come back. When I saw you guys, I followed you in. Gorgeous outfit!"

Syrinx had clammed up at Daphne's words, but Echo's heart leaped with joy to hear them. She valued her friend's loyalty, even if there was no real place for her in the forest anymore.

"Ahem! This is a closed set," Narcissus called

to them with a superior smile. "Only modeling staff allowed. Could you guys leave?"

How could she ever have crushed on this guy? Echo fumed silently. She and her friends had as much right to be here as he did. Which was to say, no right at all. This maze was equally off-limits to both mortals and nymphs. However, all she could reply to him was, "Leave?"

Pan had been glowering at Narcissus. But suddenly a mischievous grin came over his face. "Hey! Is that a pimple on your nose?" he called to the handsome boy.

The smile abruptly left Narcissus's face. Looking horrified at the possibility, he leaned down, pushed aside the reeds, bright white flowers, and lilies that grew in the pool, and then gazed worriedly at the water.

Tiresias gasped, lunging to stop him. "Wait! The prophecy!"

"Yeah! Your heart!" yelled Anaxandra.

"What pr-pr-prophecy?" Pan bleated in confusion, since he'd known nothing about it. But it was too late to take back his practical joke. Narcissus's blue eyes had found his own reflection in the pool.

"Oh doom! Certain doom!" Tiresias began wailing.

Echo bit her lip. Along with Narcissus's friends, she anxiously studied the boy. Was his heart about to vanish, as the prophecy had foretold? Although she was angry with him, she certainly didn't wish for something so tragic to happen.

However, as moments passed, Narcissus seemed fine, happy in fact. Staring at his reflection in the water, he turned his head from side to side. "Wow, I'm even handsomer than I thought."

"So your heart's okay?" Tiresias asked carefully.

"Perfect! Still beating. And no pimple," Narcissus replied. He moved his head slightly, as if intending to look over at them all, but the vain boy couldn't seem to shift his gaze from his own reflection.

"No way, mortal-dude! I don't know about your heart, but I can see tha-a-at pimple all the way from here," Pan teased.

"That's a lie! Don't listen to him, Narcissus. You look fab," insisted Tiresias. Syrinx nodded vigorously.

Ignoring them, Narcissus smiled at himself and leaned closer to his reflection. And closer. Just then a nut fell from one of the trees above them and landed on the Drakon's head, causing a random shower of small sparks to shoot forth from the beast's eyes. *Pzzzt!*

"Ow!" Sparks zinged the back of Narcissus's tunic!

Startled, he toppled headfirst into the pool. *Splash!*

When he stumbled back out, his hair was plastered to his head. Lily pads were stuck to his cheeks, and reeds were sticking out of his hair. "Nobody panic. I'm okay," he announced, as if the whole world's happiness hinged on the state of his well-being.

Hearing his pompous words and remembering what he'd said about FirHeart and "no harm done," Echo forever lost any remaining feelings she might have had for him.

Anaxandra put down her feather pen and tried to show the drawing on her papyrus scroll to Narcissus as he climbed out of the pool. "I got my sketch done just as you fell in, but those white flowers in the pool kind of got in the way, see?"

Without glancing at her or the drawing, Narcissus said, "Send it off to the reporters pronto! The sooner they get it, the sooner my dream of being asked to model is sure to come true."

"I'm on it. We're done here. Let's go!" said Tiresias. He and Anaxandra started to leave the maze, then stopped when Narcissus didn't budge. Even when he'd stumbled out of the water, his eyes had never left his reflection, Echo realized.

"C'mon," Tiresias urged him. He began to look concerned when Narcissus continued gazing into the pool, his eyes glued to his reflection on its surface.

Syrinx approached him worriedly. "Sure you're all right?"

"Are you kidding?" Narcissus smiled sweetly. "I'm in love."

"Really?" Syrinx asked, looking thrilled and obviously hoping he meant with her. Without a doubt, she was *sooo* crushing on him.

Narcissus nodded. "Yeah! I've discovered the true love of my life—*me*!"

Syrinx's face fell. "Huh?" she squeaked in surprise.

"That's it!" said Tiresias, snapping his fingers. "The prophecy *did* come true! I just remembered. It actually said your heart would be *lost*—not that it would disappear—if you saw your reflection. And you have in fact lost it . . . to yourself!"

Narcissus smiled. "Yes, isn't it wonderful?"

Echo, Pan, and Daphne looked at one another and rolled their eyes. "I hope you and your reflection will be very happy together," Pan quipped.

Though she couldn't voice her agreement, Echo giggled. Knowing Narcissus as she did now, she had a feeling that he was never going to crush on anyone but himself. He used the people around him like stair steps, leaving them behind as he scrambled ever higher. They were only a means to an end, meant to admire him and ensure the success of his modeling career.

"C'mon, Narcissus," Tiresias urged again. Then he added an enticement. "Tell you what. Now that the danger of that prophecy has passed, we can stop by the nearest agora and buy some mirrors!"

This drew Narcissus's attention. With a supreme effort he wrested his eyes from his reflection. Blowing a farewell kiss at his own image, he called out to it, "I'll miss you, buddy. See you soon!" Looking excited, he took off for the exit.

"Good-bye forever!" Echo called after him as he and his friends dashed out of the maze. Her voice echoed around the courtyard, loud and strong. Then she gasped and grinned big. The copycake spell had fallen away at last!

A sketch of Narcissus lay forgotten by the pool, and Syrinx picked it up. Clutching it to her chest, she gazed after him longingly, seeming unsure whether she should follow. But then she dropped the scroll, and her expression turned scared. "Beasts! Th-there," she whispered, backing away. She was right! Red eyes were suddenly peering out of the hedges on all sides.

"Artemis said that disturbing the Pool of Magic would disturb the beasts around here. But the three-headed fountain is the key to turning them off," Echo said, remembering.

"Then do it!" said Syrinx.

Pan nodded. "Yeah, hurry!"

"I don't know how," said Echo.

Daphne shook her head helplessly too.

Roar! Roar! As the red eyes moved closer, Syrinx

grabbed a hollow reed that grew in the fountain's waters. Sticking one end of it into her mouth, she closed her lips around it. Then she stepped into the pool, lay on her back, and submerged till she disappeared and only the end of the reed remained visible.

"She's hiding, breathing through that hollow reed like a straw! It's a river nymph trick," said Daphne.

"Good idea. Let's copy her," Echo said. Quickly she broke off three more reeds, each about a foot long, and passed them out. The three friends put their reed straws between their lips and then lay down on their backs in the pool just like Syrinx, with the tips of their reeds sticking up above the water.

The four lay silently as beast after beast lumbered through the courtyard. In the waning light their frightful, monstrous shadows fell over the pool as each passed by. Echo could make out the shape of a one-headed, two-armed, three-bodied, four-winged, six-legged Geryon. And was that a fire-breathing griffon? *Yikes!*

Luckily, however, their four breathing reeds looked exactly like any of the other reeds growing in the water, and the beasts eventually left the court-yard. When all seemed quiet, Pan peeked out. "All clear," he called to the girls.

Phew! Echo and the others sat up, dripping wet. An interesting humming sound issued from the hollow reed she held when she started to pull it from her mouth.

Pan's head swung around to look at her as they all stood up in the fountain. "Hey! Do that again."

"What, this?" Echo put one end of the reed up to—but not directly into—her mouth and sighed, causing the humming sound again.

"Pretty," said Daphne, smiling. "It sounds happy."

"Yeah," said Pan. "I never thought of blowing across the opening of a reed instead of blowing into it." There was a note of excitement in his voice. Quickly he plucked a half dozen more reeds of different lengths from the pool.

After they all climbed out of the water, he lay the reeds side by side, arranged from long to short, on the flat edge of the fountain. Then he tied them together like that using strands of lily pad vine.

"Now to test out my new instrument," he said, picking it up in both hands. By blowing across the pipes' openings as he slid them across his lips from one side of his mouth to the other, he created a tune with beautiful harmony. A smile came to his face. He waved the pipes in the air and hopped around joyfully. "It's like playing a bunch of flutes all at once. This is the sound I've been looking for!"

ROARRR! Stomp! Stomp! Stomp!

"Oh, thanks a lot, Your Loudness!" Syrinx hissed at him. "Those beasts are coming back. They must've heard you shouting!" It was too late to hide this time. The beasts had spotted them and were stomping closer and closer to the pool.

"Play your pipes, Pan," urged Echo. "Music soothes savage beasts—that's what the treechers say. Though I think they might've just gotten that idea from a play about a bride."

"Worth a try," said Pan. He raised the pipes to his mouth, blew across their openings, and slid them from side to side, creating a lively melodious tune.

Soon, goofy grins appeared on the beasts' faces. "They're smiling!" said Daphne.

"Keep playing. Don't stop!" said Echo.

Pan kept playing. Within minutes the music-bemused beasts lay down in the courtyard, curled up contentedly, and began to snore.

Once it seemed safe, Syrinx edged toward the exit. "I am *so* out of here. You can all keep your dumb forest. It's too dangerous for me. I'm off to the river. Bye!" With that, she ran out of the maze.

Echo would have been lying if she'd said she was sorry to see the disagreeable nymph go. Instead she said to her friends, "We'd better get going too, before these monsters wake up."

11

The Wedding Chiton

So ARE YOU COMING BACK TO YOUR TREE . . . ER . . .
hut?" Daphne asked Echo once they were safely out
of the maze. Her brow wrinkled and she looked
worried that her slipup might make Echo sad by
reminding her that FirHeart was no more.

Echo did feel an ache in her chest, but she managed to shrug as she twisted the hem of her soggy
bridal chiton to wring water out of it. "It's okay.

You can say 'FirHeart' without upsetting me," she said, not wanting her friend to feel bad. She didn't tell Daphne that she wasn't exactly sure where she belonged now. Instead she explained, "First I'd better go let Zeus know about the beasts, so he can get them turned off." And afterward maybe she could also figure out a way to fix things with Hera now that she wasn't copycat speaking any more.

"I'll come with you," offered Pan.

"Me too," said Daphne. She looked at Echo. "Your winged sandals are fast enough to get us to MOA and back by tonight."

"Okay," said Echo. But then she and Pan discovered that their sandals' wings, which were now soaking wet, wouldn't flap. "Bees' wings don't work well in rain, either," Echo commented. "Probably the same idea."

"Daphne, you go home so you'll be here in the morning to renew your chant for LaurelRing," Pan suggested. "I'll go with Echo just in case more beasts show up. We'll walk till our sandals dry out, then fly the rest of the way."

Daphne reluctantly agreed, and they split up, moving in opposite directions. As Echo and Pan headed back to MOA, Pan practiced playing his new pipes. Hearing his music, birds, deer, and squirrels wandered near now and then to keep them company. As she walked along, Echo's thoughts returned to Ide. Was there a way to help her? If so, that might make Hera a little bit happier too.

"I'm trying to come up with an idea for a bridal chiton," she told Pan when he took a break from playing. "Something that's not an exact copy of someone else's design."

"Sorry," said Pan. "I know zero about fashion. I just buy whatever tunic looks comfortable at the agora." But after another moment he added, "Here's a thought, though. Maybe you could use your own special *unique* fashion ideas to change an existing design." He held up his new pipes. "Like how cutting reeds into different lengths and binding them together was my own unique idea. But playing them in the same way as a flute was an existing idea that you reminded me of. Get it?"

Echo nodded. "I think so." That was probably what the treechers had been trying to get her to do in that armor assignment. But what unique ideas did she have? The answer came to her right away when a pinecone crunched underfoot. "I know. I'm really good at making fashions using forest materials!"

Pan cocked his head. "Awesome! So would the

bride you're designing for want a chiton made out of forest materials?"

"Uh, I'm not sure," Echo admitted. "The only thing I really know about her is that she cries a lot."

"Maybe you should make her chiton out of tissues, then," said Pan. They both laughed.

"Speaking of watery stuff, I think our sandals are dry," said Echo. Sitting on a log to unleash the wings on hers, she looked up at the clouds. Idly she recalled how all the nymphs she and the other goddessgirls had visited in various realms had worn outfits that seemed to fit their personalities or the places they lived.

Bzzz-bzzz. Just then a bee buzzed past her ear. It was probably off to its hive, carrying pollen to make honey. *Honey!* Suddenly it hit her in a flash. An idea for a bridal chiton. One that would look perfect on

Ide and would suit her personality to a T—or a B, as in "bee."

This time when she and Pan stood up, the wings on their sandals were dry enough to flap, and the two friends rose to hover a few inches above the ground. As they zoomed off together, the wedding gown Echo had in mind took form in her brain. She kept refining her mental picture as they flew onward.

Now and then she paused to gather objects she would need to create it. Since the borrowed chiton she wore was already a mess, she had no qualms about ripping off its upper layer of tulle to use as a net bag to carry the items she was collecting. By the time they neared the Immortal Marketplace, she had clearly visualized her bridal chiton's design.

"Whoa!" said Pan, slowing to gaze around at the IM. "Look at the crowds!"

"Wow! You're right," said Echo. "The marketplace looks jam-packed." People were coming and going, most carrying shopping bags. Despite the float fiasco, it seemed that business was picking up.

Just then Apollo and Ares flew out of the IM wearing winged sandals. Echo and Pan zipped over to them to see what was going on.

"Thanks to some kind of dramatic argument on Zeus's float, that parade generated a lot more publicity than the stores here ever dared hope for," Apollo told them. "Word of mouth brought tons of shoppers. Cassandra and her family are swamped with cookie orders in the bakery too."

"Yeah," said Ares. "Mighty Fighty was so full we couldn't even get in. We're heading home till the crowds die down some, if they ever do."

When the two godboys finally noticed their soggy

clothes, Echo and Pan explained about the beasts. Apollo and Ares quickly offered to accompany them to Mount Olympus to get help from Zeus. But Pan waved Echo off into the IM, saying, "Go! You need to see Hera. We'll ta-ta-take care of the beasts."

After thanking the three boys and wishing them well on their errand, Echo swooped over and entered the IM. Inside, she borrowed a graphite stick and a sheet of papyrus from the Oracle-O Bakery and Scrollbooks. It wasn't easy to find an empty table in the bustling atrium, but she managed, and sat to quickly sketch out her bridal chiton idea while it was still fresh in her mind.

Once she finished it, she regarded it critically. To her eye it was perfect. But would Ide think so? She would give it to Hera and let her be the judge. If it wasn't too late, that was. For all she knew, Ide had given the shop a second chance and Hera herself might've already created a new bridal chiton for her.

Leaving the atrium, Echo headed for Hera's Happy Endings with her net bag of forest materials and her sketch. When she entered the shop, she saw that Melissa, Amalthea, and Ide were there with Hera and her assistants. They were all gathered in the center of the store, earnestly discussing the problem of how to replace Ide's bridal chiton. Their voices were tense, as if there were major disagreements among them. Ide sounded especially upset.

"Um, excuse me," said Echo, drawing their attention. They all stared at her in surprise. Probably partly because her chiton looked so bedraggled by now, but also because they never expected her to have the nerve to show her face again.

"You! You ruined everything," Ide accused right away.

Though she understood how Ide must feel, Echo plowed ahead. "I've brought something. I know it won't excuse what happened earlier today, but it's a sketch for a new bridal chiton. For you, if you like it." She held out her sketch, but Ide refused to accept it.

However, Amalthea and Hera took the sketch and gazed at it with interest. "Hmm. I never thought of using honeycombs," said Hera. They handed the sketch to Melissa, who brightened when she saw it and insisted that her daughter view it. When Ide finally, reluctantly turned her face toward the sketch, she froze.

Echo cringed, thinking the worst. She had done her best to fix things. But she'd obviously been barking up the wrong tree with her idea. "I'm sorry you don't like it." She turned to go. But a gentle hand touched her arm, staying her. It was Ide!

"Th-thank you," Ide gasped between happy tears. "It's . . . p-p-perfect!"

Echo looked at her in consternation.

"Ide's right. It's inspired. And it *is* perfect for her," said Melissa. "But is there time to make it?" Everyone looked at Hera.

"I have most of the materials here, but some of the items will need to come from the forest. I'm not sure how long it will take to gather them," said Hera.

Echo held up her tulle bag. "Got it covered. On my way here I collected some abandoned honeycombs and leaves and other stuff we might need."

"Oh! You are a darling!" said Melissa, giving her a hug. "So you'll help?"

"Well, I kind of need to change clothes first," Echo

said, glancing down at her bedraggled chiton. Hera quickly loaned her a fresh one from one of the racks.

As they all five worked together with the shop assistants, Echo explained to Hera everything that she'd been unable to explain while under the spell of the copycake. "I'm sorry I took outfits from your shop," she apologized. "Narcissus told me that Zeus had invited us to join you on the float and that we'd be helping your shop by modeling clothes from it. I believed him, but what I did was still wrong."

"I'd guessed as much, and you are forgiven," Hera replied graciously. "You see, I found Ide's actual bridal chiton in our alterations room a few minutes ago and realized you hadn't taken it. It's unfortunate that Narcissus lied and shifted the blame to you. Some people only think of themselves."

Wasn't that the truth!

With so many hands to help, the new chiton was completed by sunset. As Ide tried it on for a final fitting, a winged news-scroll banged against the door of the shop. When one of the assistants opened the door, the news-scroll flew in.

"The lead article is about the IM!" the assistant enthused after scanning it. "I bet we'll get even more shoppers here next week!" She handed the news-scroll to Hera.

"Look!" Hera said to Echo. "There's a drawing of you and Narcissus jumping out of the cake on our float." But before showing Echo the picture, Hera unrolled more of the scroll. "And here's another of him in the Forest of the Beasts in a different article."

Echo peeked at the drawings and grinned. In the one that accompanied the first article, titled "Immortal Marketplace Parade Takes the Cake!", her upraised arm was accidentally covering the vain boy's handsome face. He would not be at all happy about that.

The caption for the second drawing read: BEASTS GO WILD AS NARCISSUS MAKES A SPLASH. He'd been drawn at the very moment when he'd toppled into the pool, so you couldn't see his face in this one either. In fact the focus of the drawing seemed to be a bunch of bright white flowers growing in the fountain.

"'Narcissus,'" read Ide, looking over Echo's shoulder. "Is that the name of those white flowers? They're so pretty. I must carry some in my wedding bouquet!"

"I know exactly where to find them," Echo replied, not bothering to correct Ide's mistake. She quickly explained to Hera that the requested flowers grew in a pool inside a labyrinth where Zeus was probably headed right now to turn off some beasts.

"No problem," said Hera. "I'll send a magic breeze asking him to pick some and bring them back for a bouquet. Anything to make Ide's wedding perfect!" As Ide hugged and thanked Echo, it seemed that all was forgiven.

Monday arrived, the day of Ide's wedding. Guests gathered in the Immortal Marketplace atrium to witness the ceremony. Echo was thrilled to have been invited too. Along with other wedding attendees, she sat in one of the many white chairs that had been set up in rows on either side of a center aisle.

When the wedding march music began to play, courtesy of Apollo and his talented friends in Heavens Above, Echo and everyone else stood and turned to look for the bride. As Ide appeared at the far end of the aisle, there were gasps.

"What a beautiful chiton!" someone murmured.

"She looks fantastic!" said another.

"Extraordinary!" put in a third.

The new chiton Echo had designed did look perfect on Ide. It was long and white with a delicate honey-colored netting overlay. White flower petals clung to its bodice, and teardrops of tree pitch sparkled among them. Here and there honeycombs dyed white had been artfully placed on the skirt, while magical honeybees held her long veil to flare out behind her. As Ide passed Echo, she winked, and Echo grinned back.

Murmurs of pleased admiration followed the bride as she slowly moved up the aisle toward her groom and Zeus. The two men, who stood under a tall arch among rhododendron bushes and fountains, smiled broadly at Ide's approach.

"What kind of flowers are those she's carrying?" Echo heard someone ask.

"They're called Narcissus. I saw them in a drawing in a *Greekly Weekly* article," another guest answered.

Despite all the trouble he'd caused, Echo felt kind of bad about Narcissus missing his big chance at stardom. However, at least his name was getting famous. Even if people thought it referred to a white flower instead of to him.

As Zeus began to speak the words that would officially marry the couple, the sweet notes of Pan's new reed pipes filled the atrium. At Echo's suggestion Ide had invited the shepherd godboy to play quietly in the background during the actual ceremony, after Apollo's band had finished the wedding march.

Echo saw Apollo's head jerk around to gaze at Pan,

and there was enthusiastic interest in his face. She had a feeling Pan had found the sound he needed to be allowed to jam with Heavens Above!

When both bride and groom said "I do," Ide began crying happy tears. Which made Zeus look a little nervous. He spoke quickly after that, and the wedding was soon over. To the sounds of laughter and cheers, the happy couple was whisked away to begin their honeymoon, in a white chariot pulled by honey-colored horses.

Afterward there were snacks and festivities as the crowd lingered. Echo wound up hanging out with Athena, Artemis, Aphrodite, Persephone, and some of their crushes.

"Do brides always cry?" she heard Ares ask Heracles.

Overhearing, Zeus answered, "No, but they can be cranky in the days leading up to their wedding."

"Are you saying I was cranky before our wedding?" asked Hera, whose arm was linked with his.

"Oh no, sweetie pie," he hastened to say. "I just . . . That is . . . You've told me yourself that brides often cry in your shop."

"So that's why there's always a box of tissues on every table in your stepmom's store!" Echo heard Artemis whisper to Athena. Athena nodded.

Hera patted Zeus's arm. "I'm just teasing, dear. Brides have been known to cry all kinds of tears, but mostly excited and happy ones. I've seen a few grooms shed a tear or two as well." She eyed him.

Zeus gave a small, embarrassed-sounding cough. "Ahem, well, enough of that." Which made them all laugh.

Now Hera nudged him and nodded toward Echo.

"Huh?" Zeus said. But after a moment he seemed

250

to remember something. "Oh yeah," he said to Echo at last. "Hera told me that your little surprise on our float has brought shoppers out to the Immortal Marketplace in droves. And that in the end you saved the day for Ide. In view of your tremendous help, I say let's stick with our original plan. I'll help you relocate to another realm as a different kind of nymph."

"Have you chosen what kind you want to become?" asked Athena. She and her friends looked at Echo with interest.

Without hesitation Echo blurted, "A fashion design nymph."

Artemis looked perplexed. "There's no such thing."

"What I mean is, I've decided I want to study fashion design," Echo explained. When everyone just looked at her blankly, her heart sank. She could hardly blame them for their reaction, though. Nymphs just didn't do such things. So she had no real role model to follow—in other words, no one to copy. Becoming a fashion design nymph was an even more *unique* idea than using honeycombs in her design of Ide's gown!

At last Hera tapped a fingertip on her chin. "Hmm. A famous designer on Earth named Moda contacted me recently to say that he's holding a competition for students to work under his tutelage. He suggested that I submit for consideration a portfolio of the work of any promising young designers. If you have additional sketches of ideas as original as Ide's gown, I can promise to send them his way."

For a few seconds hope bloomed in Echo. This was the chance of a lifetime. If she became the first-ever nymph fashion designer, *she'd* be an original. But all of her sketches had gotten ruined in the FirHeart disaster. Besides, her old ideas—including the pattern for the dress she'd worn on the float—were only copies of stuff she'd seen in *Teen Scrollazine* or *Greekly Weekly* or Hera's idea book. She didn't think Moda would be interested in a copycat designer.

"No," she replied sadly. "No sketches. No ideas."

12

New Beginnings

AFTER THE WEDDING RECEPTION ECHO RELUC-
tantly returned home to the Boeotian forest. She'd
been gone for several days now and wondered if
she'd be accepted back among the other nymphs.
Especially since she'd have to remain treeless. There
was one positive thing. At least Syrinx had gone back
to her river.

Dusk was falling as Echo arrived, moving through

the woods. One by one the forest nymphs began to peek out from behind the tree trunks and between branches, their pale faces glowing like fairy lights. To her surprise they had come out to greet her.

"Welcome home!" they called out in their sweet voices. The Syrinx effect seemed to have faded. Her friends were back to being her friends!

As she went deeper into the forest, a full moon rose to light her way. Soon Daphne ran over to hug her and hand her a messagescroll. "This just came for you." Since messages didn't often come to the forest, their friends gathered around, curious to find out who it was from and what it was about.

Echo unrolled the scroll. She scanned it quickly, joy rising inside her at what she read. "It's from Hera!" She grinned big. "Turns out she sent Moda—this *evergreen* fashion designer—a sketch I made for

Zeus's nanny's daughter Ide's bridal chiton. When Hera told Moda it was my idea, he offered to take me on as an apprentice, even though it's just one design. He's going to send me assignments, and Hera has offered to help me with them. I'm supposed to go to her shop one day a week for a class. I'm so happy!" Echo began jumping around in delight.

"But you'll live here with us again, right?" Daphne asked anxiously.

Echo nodded, pleased that her BFF so obviously wanted her back. "Since my ideas spring from nature, Moda wants me to stay in the forest to inspire my future creations. He says it'll be my *brand*."

This all felt right to her. The forest was where she'd be happiest, she knew. And yet this wonderful news didn't change the fact that she was still treeless. Nothing ever would.

Smiling now, Daphne exchanged a look of excitement with the other nymphs. "Come," she said to Echo. "We've got something to show you." She and the others began to lead Echo in the direction of her hut and the stump that had once been her beloved FirHeart.

Echo dragged her heels a little. She wasn't really looking forward to this. It would be painful to see the stump. Yet she had missed her tree and yearned to be near the place it had stood again. Her feelings were so mixed up!

Once they arrived at her old home, she could scarcely bring herself to look. When she finally mustered up the courage to do so, she gasped. Her friends had tidied up the area around her hut and added decorations to make it cute! They'd tucked berries and cones around the outside of the hut and donated things to make it homier. There was a new rug woven from bark strips on the hut's swept dirt floor, a shell vase with flowers on her table, pictures on the walls, and a new hammock and quilt. A dozen homemade candles sat here and there, bringing golden light.

"Thanks, you guys!" said Echo. "It's b-beautiful!" Overwhelmed with joy and gratitude, tears welled up in her eyes. The way she was feeling, she was going to need some of Hera's shop's tissues pretty soon.

"That's not all," said Daphne. "Look!" She led Echo around to the back side of the stump.

Echo had avoided looking at it, but now she did as directed. At first she wasn't sure what her BFF wanted her to see. But then . . . slowly . . . Echo realized there was something new amid the lovely arrangement of foliage her friends had created around FirHeart's roots.

"A sapling!" she breathed, scarcely daring to believe her eyes. It had grown up from the stump!

As she bent and gently touched it, the tears in her eyes finally overflowed. With wet cheeks she straightened to look up at her gathered friends. "This is the most evergreen gift of nature ever . . . I can't believe it!"

Suddenly, a giggle escaped her as a thought occurred. Then she started laughing through her tears. Her friends gazed at her in curious surprise. "Syrinx used to call me a copycat," she explained. "Now it looks like my tree is a copycat too! It copied itself. Sort of."

At this, her friends started giggling too, and soon everyone was laughing.

"With the enchantments you say each morning, this sapling will grow extra fast," said Daphne. "And till its full grown, you can live with me or in your hut, whichever you choose."

"Thanks. You guys are the best!" Echo said, gazing around at everyone. "You've made this little hut so adorable! It'll be the perfect home for me to watch over FirHeart Junior as he grows up."

Silently she vowed to watch over this sapling well. With her care it would grow strong and tall. Within a few years it would be big enough to build in. And build she would, creating another house high in its branches. And in the meantime she'd have her class with Hera, which she was sooo excited about. Things were really looking up!

Daphne and the other nymphs hugged Echo and then eventually drifted away one by one. After they were gone, Echo kneeled before FirHeart Junior once more. With her hands gently cupping the sapling, she murmured her chant for the very first time to this new tree-to-be, solemnly and joyfully promising to guard it from this day forward:

> *"Protect this tree.*
>
> *Let no ax chop it.*
>
> *Should trouble come,*
>
> *Let my spell stop it.*
>
> *Through happy times*
>
> *Or stormy weather,*
>
> *Let nymph and tree*
>
> *forever be . . .*
>
> *together."*

Don't miss the next adventure in
the Goddess Girls series!

Coming Soon